"Come here," Noah said, reaching out to her. "Take my hand. We'll go back to the car together. I promise I won't leave you again."

She hesitated, then placed her palm in his. Heat infused his skin, racing up his arm. Noah knew, as he pulled Victoria toward him, that leaving this city, this woman, wasn't going to be simple. No, this tie was becoming more and more tangled by the minute.

"Thank you," she said again after they'd made their way to a quieter section of the street. "I got a little swamped by the crowds."

A little swamped? He didn't say it, but to his eyes she looked as if she'd been caught in a storm. He held tight to her hand, keeping her close as they made their way back to where her car was parked.

The woman beside him was a reality that Noah hadn't counted on. His best-laid plans had just been disrupted—by his own heart.

D0366147

Dear Reader,

This book was probably one of my most challenging to write, and certainly an experience I will never forget. Because, in the middle of writing about Victoria's loss, I lost my own mother.

I think, just as Victoria says, that losing someone so close to you changes you forever. I know it has impacted the way I look at the world, how tightly I hug my children, and also how and what I write.

Although there were many days after my mother died that I couldn't write, ultimately I realized that putting my words on paper and bringing my books to readers was the best testament I could give her. She was always so proud of me, and would brag about her "daughter the author" to everyone from the UPS driver to her hairdresser. She would have wanted me to press on, to finish this book and then write another. And another.

I hope that you, dear reader, will persevere in whatever is important to you. That you, too, will treasure each day and the gifts that come with every sunrise. And always remember to make each moment count and hold dear those around you.

Shirley

Rescued
by Mr. Right

SHIRLEY JUMP

SILHOUETTE *Romance*®
Published by Silhouette Books
America's Publisher of Contemporary Romance

If you purchased this book without a cover you should be aware that this book is stolen property. It was reported as "unsold and destroyed" to the publisher, and neither the author nor the publisher has received any payment for this "stripped book."

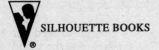 SILHOUETTE BOOKS

ISBN-13: 978-0-373-19834-4
ISBN-10:   0-373-19834-5

RESCUED BY MR. RIGHT

First North American Publication 2006

Copyright © 2006 by Shirley Kawa-Jump

All rights reserved. Except for use in any review, the reproduction or utilization of this work in whole or in part in any form by any electronic, mechanical or other means, now known or hereafter invented, including xerography, photocopying and recording, or in any information storage or retrieval system, is forbidden without the written permission of the editorial office, Silhouette Books, 233 Broadway, New York, NY 10279 U.S.A.

All characters in this book have no existence outside the imagination of the author and have no relation whatsoever to anyone bearing the same name or names. They are not even distantly inspired by any individual known or unknown to the author, and all incidents are pure invention.

This edition published by arrangement with Harlequin Books S.A.

® and TM are trademarks of Harlequin Books S.A., used under license. Trademarks indicated with ® are registered in the United States Patent and Trademark Office, the Canadian Trade Marks Office and in other countries.

Visit Silhouette Books at www.eHarlequin.com

Printed in U.S.A.

SHIRLEY JUMP

Bookseller's Best Award-winner Shirley Jump didn't have the willpower to diet, nor the talent to master under-eye concealer, so she bowed out of a career in television and opted instead for a career where she could be paid to eat at her desk—writing. At first, seeking revenge on her children for their grocery-store tantrums, she sold embarrassing essays about them to anthologies. However, it wasn't enough to feed her growing addiction to writing. So she turned to the world of romance novels, where messes are (usually) cleaned up before "The End" and no one is calling anyone a doodoo head. In the worlds Shirley gets to create and control, the children listen to their parents, the husbands always remember holidays and the housework is magically done by elves. Though she's thrilled to see her books in stores around the world, Shirley mostly writes because it gives her an excuse to avoid cleaning the toilets and it helps feed her shoe-shopping habit. To learn more, visit her Web site at www.shirleyjump.com

Look out for Shirley's Harlequin NEXT book, THE OTHER WIFE, coming in November.

Join Penny Reynolds on her journey to discover her late husband's secrets. Finding the other wife was a surprise enough, but when she meets the infamous Harvey the Wonder Dog and is introduced to the crazy world of dog shows, she starts to realize that she didn't really know her husband at all…and is forced to ask how well she really knows herself.

You can read more of Shirley's books coming in 2007 from Harlequin Romance

To my mother, who wasn't just "Momma,"
she was one of my best friends, too. I will miss
your voice, your hugs and most of all, you.

CHAPTER ONE

THE next time he ran away from his life, Noah McCarty vowed to make a better plan—or at least give it more forethought than a six-year-old staging a walkout over the lima beans.

Normally he wasn't a man given to impetuous acts. Anyone who knew him would agree—spontaneity definitely wasn't his strong suit. It wasn't even a shirt in his closet.

Through the mud-spotted windshield, steam rose from the radiator in an angry, sputtering cloud. The pickup he'd never had time to bring into the shop had finally quit on him. He cursed several times, feeling his annoyance build with every vapor cloud.

This was the last straw in an already small haystack.

He couldn't blame the truck. For the better part of the morning, they'd been battling Friday morning stop-and-go traffic on I-93. Finally, in frustration, Noah had gotten off on one of the exits, figuring the scenic route would be better than crawling along at a caterpillar's pace.

Noah had gotten lost, ending up journeying along

Quincy Shore Drive, heading nowhere. With no one waiting for his arrival, no one even knowing where he'd gone, he had the luxury of dawdling. As he drove into Hough's Neck, the roads narrowed, the area becoming less city-stepchild and more remote further down the peninsula.

Until the truck had shuddered to a halt, refusing to go another inch further.

In front of him, the radiator continued to spit and hiss, disturbing the quiet of the beachside street. Noah got out of the Silverado, stretching his arms over his head, releasing the kinks in his back. It didn't work. The kinks had become a permanent part of him, like an extra benefit for his job.

Aches, pains and heartbreak—all part of the joys of working in the juvenile justice system. Those were the bonuses he received to offset the awful pay, even worse hours and—

He wasn't going to think about that. When he got to Maine, he was going to hole up in Mike's cabin for a few days and have a damned fine pity party.

Because Noah McCarty had failed. In a very big way.

The only thing he could do was retreat, lick his wounds and then come up with a career that involved absolutely no contact with human beings. Mountain climber. Sewer unplugger. Professional hermit. Yeah, his career options were limitless.

Either way, when he returned to Providence, he was done being the patron of lost causes.

From his place inside the cab, Charlie, his mother's well-indulged pocket pet, stopped shredding the Chevy's dash and let out a woof. Well, what passed for a woof coming from a voice box the size of a dime. Noah turned, then saw what had attracted the Chihuahua's canine instincts.

A woman.

Not just *a* woman, but a beautiful woman. She stood on the porch of a small white Dutch Colonial, the breeze toying with her dark brown hair and tangling it around a heart-shaped face with eyes so blue they seemed to be part of the ocean behind the property. The scenery around the woman could have been an ad in a travel magazine. Parts of the oceanfront land were still untamed, with sea grass growing in wild spurts among the sand and driftwood. It was a warm September day, picturesque and perfect.

She was watching him, a sign in her hands, a question on her lips. The sign was turned to the side, but he could still read the hand-lettered words.

Room for Rent.

The ocean breeze skipped across the beach and up the walk, whispering its salty breath beneath Noah's nose. He inhaled, and when he did, he brought into his chest the scent of the open water. Of freedom.

Of exactly what he'd been looking for.

"Room for Rent," he read again. Perhaps he didn't need to travel all the way to Maine for his personal misery party.

But just as quickly as he had the thought, he dismissed it. Mike's cabin was isolated, uninhabited. The perfect escape for a man who had every intention of becoming a grumpy recluse for a while.

"Can I help you?" she asked, taking a step forward, shading her eyes with a palm.

"My truck broke down." He thumbed in the direction of the Chevy. "Could I use your phone? I'd call a tow truck myself but my cell battery is dead, too." Irony, in its finest form. All at the same time, his career, his reputation, his vehicle and most of his major electronic gadgets had imploded.

His mother, who believed anything coming out of a fortune cookie was gospel, would say it was a sign. A sign of what, he didn't know.

"Where were you going?"

"Maine."

A slight smile crossed her face. "Maine. I've never been there."

"That's something we have in common." He took a few steps forward, bringing his waist into contact with the short white slats of the gate. A white picket fence, he mused. The stereotype of home.

A stereotype that didn't exist, something Noah knew too damned well.

"Noah McCarty," he said, thrusting out a hand. This wasn't involvement. It was being polite.

She hesitated, still clutching the sign to her chest, then after a second, took a step forward, as hesitant as a baby bird. When her hand met his, warmth infused his palm, skating up his veins.

"Victoria Blackstone," she said, her voice as quiet as the light, teasing wind. She released his palm, then unlatched the gate to let him in. But as he slid through the two-foot opening, he noticed a wariness in her eyes, an uncertainty in her movements, and realized how he must look, stepping out of his beat-up truck.

That morning, he'd left his apartment in a hurry,

without shaving or taking the time to don anything more complicated than a pair of old, paint-stained jeans and a raggedy T-shirt he'd gotten free at some festival.

"Nice to meet you," he said, to show her that his mother had raised him with a few manners.

"Come on in. You're welcome to use my phone."

"I appreciate it."

As they started up the walk, she glanced down at his boots, caked with mud from a foray into the woods two days ago. A trip that had been unsuccessful, resulting in Noah knee-deep in the soggy earth and his nephew, Justin, gone, as if he'd disappeared into the ether. "Do you mind wiping your feet? I have this thing about dirt on the floor."

A woman with rules. He hadn't met one of those since he'd left home at fifteen. "Will do. And I promise not to sneeze on the receiver or belch aloud or do anything else that might be even remotely disgusting or male."

A smile spread across her face. It wasn't an ordinary smile, the kind you saw on strangers passing you on the street. Or the kind people gave when they were handed a fruitcake at Christmas. It was a smile that had legs, one that softened into her cheeks and raised them into bright apple shapes.

The kind of genuine smile Noah hadn't seen in a long, long time.

A slight blush whispered over her features. She turned away and continued up her walkway. Behind him, Noah heard a familiar patter of itty-bitty paws.

Oh, no. The dog.

Before Noah could grab him, Charlie hurried past, tossing a growl at Noah as he did. Then he did a Jekyll and Hyde, shifting his demeanor to friendly. Cute, even. He darted up, thrust his nose against the bare leg beneath Victoria's capris, and introduced himself. Victoria gasped, then stopped, gaping at Charlie. "Oh my goodness. What a cute dog! Is he yours?"

If she only knew the personality lurking beneath that pixie canine face, the wolverine in Disney packaging. "Meet Charlie," Noah said, gesturing toward the pedigreed pup, who had wisely withdrawn his nose and planted his butt on the concrete beside Noah, whip-thin tail swishing loose stone dust from side to side. Looking for all the world like he might actually be a nice dog.

Ha.

"Well, hello, Charlie." When her soft gaze connected with Noah's, he thought a man could fall into those eyes as easily as a down bed. "He seems attached to you."

"Not really. He knows which side his bread is buttered on and who's got the butter." Then he recovered his manners, thought of her. "Are you allergic to dogs? If you are, I can make him wait in the truck. He snuck out because he thinks everyone loves him."

Victoria's laughter was rich and melodic, a one-person vocal orchestra. "Maybe he's never met anyone who disagrees."

"Considering the way my mother's brought him up, you might be right. She dropped him off at my house with only one instruction—indulge his every whim."

Victoria considered Charlie, the sign once again clutched to her chest. "I've never had a dog. Or a cat." She spoke so quietly, he wondered if she was including him in the conversation. "Or come to think of it, a goldfish."

"I've always had a pet, usually one I found somewhere. Before my mother left Charlie with me, it was a cat. I had Bowser for five years and before him, it was Max and Matilda, a couple of dogs who thought playing fetch was for sissies," Noah said. "I seem to be the type that attracts strays."

The words left a sharp pain in their wake. He'd done far too much of that rescuing the unrescuable thing.

"I'm sorry, I didn't even think to ask you," she said. "Would you like a glass of lemonade? Iced tea?"

It was simple hospitality, but for some reason, it hit Noah hard. Maybe it was the beautiful woman. The ocean air. The fact that he hadn't dated anyone in a long, long time. Either way, he felt something begin to stir within him, as if his old self were being resurrected.

That was crazy. He'd been out in the heat too long. Inhaled some of the radiator fumes.

"Lemonade would be great, thanks." Beside him, Charlie let out a high-pitched bark.

Victoria laughed again. "And some water for you, Charlie."

She left the sign on the porch, facing the words inward. As he scraped the soles of his boots against the welcome mat and then entered the house, he realized he'd never seen a home this tidy. She was clearly one of those women who took a scrub brush to everything in her life.

The tidiness he could understand, but the decor stopped him cold. He might as well have stepped onto the set of *Happy Days*. From the chrome kitchen set down the hall to the boxy floral sofa in the living room to his right, he could practically see the Cunninghams in every detail. Though he didn't know her well, he couldn't quite wrap his mind around the delicate, capris-clad Victoria Blackstone and these outdated rooms. "Behave yourself," he whispered to Charlie. "No peeing on her favorite chair. Or eating her shoes. Or gnawing escape hatches in the walls."

Charlie lifted his nose in the air and jaunted forward, as if he'd never consider such a thing and as if he hadn't just done all three things to Noah's apartment last night.

"The phone's over there," she said, pointing at a white wall phone in the kitchen.

"Thanks." He entered the room, noting the checker-board pattern on the linoleum and the porcelain sink that was nearly as big as a bathtub. Something simmered in a Crock-Pot on the counter, filling the room with the scent of beef. He picked up the receiver, turned it to use the underside, then paused, noticing the coiled cord and ring of numbers. "Is this an antique?"

"Antique?" She glanced at the phone, laughed, then turned back to the avocado-colored refrigerator to pull out a pitcher of lemonade. Slices of lemon danced in the pale liquid. No doubt fresh squeezed. "Probably. We've had it in the house forever. My parents were a little wary of the whole touch-tone revolution."

Wary of touch-tone phones? What century was this house living in? For a minute, Noah felt as if he'd stepped back in time, transported to the world he'd in-habited when he was a little boy. When his father had been around and dinners had been on the table every night, waiting for them to create a family at the circular table. The phone would ring, and his mother would let it go, because dinner was a sacred time. Anyone who dared interrupt it better have a damned good excuse.

When he'd been thirteen and waiting to hear from Stevie Klein if Margaret O'Neil really did like him, the whole phone thing had been an annoyance. But now, in the shadows of history, he saw it as his mother trying to preserve family togetherness.

In the end, she hadn't been able to preserve a damned thing.

Once again, Noah shook off the memories. He needed a mechanic, not a stroll down Reminiscence Lane. "Do you have a phone book? I need to call a tow truck and find a motel nearby. I'll probably need a place to stay until my truck is ready."

"Sure. Give me a second." Victoria handed him a glass of lemonade then returned to the sink to fill a plastic bowl with water for Charlie. After she turned it off, the faucet continued to drip, slow and steady. Plop. Plop. Plop.

She gave the water to Charlie, who exuded gratitude with a yip and a frantic wag of his tail. Clearly the dog preferred female caretakers.

Hell, looking at Victoria, Noah couldn't say he blamed Charlie. She leaned comfortably against the counter, her delicate features and bemused smile an odd juxtaposition to the linoleum flooring and avocado green appliances, and watched the dog take delicate, single laps from the bowl. If there was one thing Charlie despised, it was getting wet.

Behind her, he could still hear the sink drip. "You know, I can fix that for you." He gestured toward the sink, wondering what on earth had possessed him to make that offer. His plan was to tow and run, not pause for a rerun of *This Old House*. "Probably needs a new washer."

"It does. I just haven't had a chance to pick one up at the store."

He arched a brow, impressed. "A woman who knows some plumbing?"

She laughed. "I've been taking care of things around here for years. Even have my own set of tools."

"With pink handles?" He remembered seeing a set like that once in a hardware store.

"Of course." A grin spread across her face. "Wouldn't want some man coming along and thinking that hammer was his."

"You get many of them? Men trying to take your hammer?" The question, and the hint of innuendo, tumbled out of his mouth before he could stop it. Clearly he'd been working in an all-male office too long.

"Not many." She wagged a finger at him. "So don't get any ideas about my tools."

There was another innuendo in those words, something that Noah chose to ignore. He was here to use the phone, get his truck fixed…

And nothing more.

Nevertheless, "ideas" flowed through his brain without an invitation. He was, after all, a man with a pulse. Just add water and a gorgeous woman and watch those ideas grow.

"Your, ah, tool kit is safe from me," he said. "The only thing I need is my radiator fixed. Any chance your talents extend to that?"

She threw up her hands in surrender. "Nope. But I sure can call triple-A Larry."

He laughed, the sound bursting from his throat such a surprise he almost choked it back. How long had it been since he'd laughed like that? The fact that he couldn't remember told him it had been too damned long. "Well, you're in good company. I can fix a leaky faucet, even hang some Sheetrock, but I'm engine illiterate."

For a long second, she didn't say anything, her blue eyes sweeping over him, studying him as intently as a prosecutor. "So, Noah McCarty, what are you running away from?"

Bam. Just like that, she'd nailed him. He let out a startled chuckle. "Am I that transparent?"

She smiled, this time a softer, shyer version. "Not really. I just put a few pieces together. The truck. The filled duffel bag in the back. The Rhode Island plates and you mentioning Maine. And…"

"And?"

"Well…you seem like a guy who's trying to get away from something." Her cheeks filled with crimson. "I could be totally wrong, too. I'm not exactly a social butterfly, so my person-to-person skills are a bit rusty."

"You're fine." Then he scowled, mad at himself for admitting that. He'd been drawn in, even taken a half-step closer to her, to try to discover what it was about this stranger that had his heart beating faster and his brain forgetting the plan.

"I'm sorry. I tend to be blunt."

"That's okay. Really." He clutched the phone tighter, the hard plastic a stab of reality. *Get back to the point, McCarty. No lingering. No wondering who this woman is and why she's living in a time warp.* "Phone book? Or should I call information? Or…" He paused. He shouldn't say it. Should simply get on his way again as fast as possible.

"What?"

He had never seen eyes quite that color before. Big and

rich, filled with a hue of blue that varied as much as an ocean wave. He stopped himself, though, just before he ended his "or" with the words "room for rent." "Uh…nothing. Just thinking about what to do with the truck."

She pushed off from the counter and moved to straighten one of the chrome chairs, putting it back into perfect alignment with the silvery table legs. "There are plenty of auto repair shops around here, but if you want a recommendation, I'd say Larry. I've dealt with the same mechanic for years and I trust him. He'll come and get your truck, fix it for a reasonable price and not put in parts you don't need. It's the end of the day, though, so I bet he can't get to it until tomorrow. As for a motel—" she paused for a fraction of time "—if you want to stay here, I have that empty room."

Room for Rent.

How easy it would be to take Victoria up on her offer. To stay here, to let the beckoning ocean outside her window wash through his exhausted muscles. But staying here meant staying with someone. Noah's entire reason for going to Maine was to eliminate all human contact from his life.

"Thanks, but I really can't stay." He cocked a hip against the wall, the phone still in his hand. "I need to get up to—"

"I understand," she cut in suddenly. "Let me get you that phone book so you can call a motel." She headed quickly out of the room.

Charlie strolled over, plopped down beside Noah's feet and let out a sharp bark. "I take it you like her?" he asked.

The dog only looked up at him in response, his ears perking like two equilateral triangles.

"I thought you were supposed to be so picky. Evian and Iams only."

Charlie let out another of his wannabee barks, then laid down and started gnawing on the hem of Noah's jeans, content as a monkey with a banana.

"We should leave," Noah told him, raising his foot, shaking off the dog.

Undaunted, Charlie's tiny, razor sharp teeth got back to wreaking havoc. He was, after all, a dog very used to getting his own way. Not to mention a silk-lined doggy bed—which Noah had refused to take with him. If Noah was roughing it, Charlie could damned well do the same.

The idea of roughing it didn't seem quite so appealing now, though. Mike's cabin was mainly used for hunting trips and weekend stays in the summer. It didn't have electricity or running water, just a fireplace and a stack of canned goods.

Nevertheless, the cabin was ideal hermit material. The sooner Noah got there, the better. He needed some time to come up with a better plan and figure out exactly what to do about Justin.

The seconds ticked by on the black plastic cat-shaped wall clock. The faucet kept up its steady tempo. But Victoria didn't return. She couldn't get lost in her own house and the chances of her not knowing where the phone book was in such a tidy place were slim.

He told himself to remain exactly where he was, not to go look for her, because doing that would start the whole snowball of involvement.

Charlie paused in his denim snack and raised his head. "No," Noah said.

The dog let out a little bark, then tugged at Noah's

pant leg. When Noah didn't move, Charlie heaved a sigh and dropped his head onto Noah's foot. It had all the weight of a crew sock.

"Oh, all right," Noah muttered. "I'll make sure she's okay. But that doesn't mean we're staying."

He disengaged himself from the stubborn Chihuahua and headed into the opposite room. Victoria could have fallen, broken a bone, hit her head. He may be keeping his distance from humans, but that didn't mean he couldn't be relied upon for the occasional 9-1-1 event.

Yeah, right. That's exactly why he was doing this. So he could demonstrate his CPR skills.

The thought of doing mouth-to-mouth on Victoria rippled through him. He quickly pushed it away. Jeez, five minutes after meeting a beautiful woman and he was on his way to becoming Valentino.

The living room was empty. So was the bathroom. Just past the archway connecting the living room and dining room he saw her. The shades were drawn, darkening the space into a dusky indoor twilight and giving an eerie cast to the long, narrow dining room table and the matching high-backed, claw-foot chairs. The wood floors, topped with a rectangular floral carpet. Like the rest of the house, the room was a throwback to earlier days.

Victoria had her back to him, standing beside a sideboard that took up most of the wall. A parade of family photos in silver frames sat across the top of the furniture piece. Victoria's shoulders were hunched forward, her head down.

Oh, hell. Something softened in Noah's heart. Try as he might to harden it again, his best intentions dissolved the second he heard a sob escape her throat. "Victoria?"

She wheeled around, at the same time swiping at her cheek. "Sorry, I…ah…I couldn't find the phone book."

"Listen, I'll just—" He thumbed over his shoulder, intending to say, "leave," but the word lodged in his throat.

"I was looking in a drawer for it, but…" Her voice trailed off, and in the final notes, he heard the one emotion he'd vowed never to come near again.

Loss.

Noah recognized it as surely as his own name. He'd seen it, in the faces of parents who'd lost their children to drugs. He'd heard it, in the final phone call before a gunshot. He'd felt it, in courtroom after courtroom as children too young to drive were carted off to finish growing up in jail.

But most of all, he'd carried that feeling with him all the way from Rhode Island, tucked squarely inside his chest.

What the hell was he thinking? That he could go to Maine for a few days and the whispers in his mind would stop? That he could sit on a dock and fish for bass like a normal man? As if he was on vacation, not a life departure? That some cabin in the woods would be enough to make him forget such a colossal mistake?

And did he really think he could walk out of this house right now, leaving that sound hanging in Victoria Blackstone's dining room?

His feet carried him across the room, until he was close enough to see the shimmer in her eyes. "Are you okay?"

"Fine. Really." Her smile trembled on her lips.

As easily as putting on a pair of jeans, Noah slipped into his familiar work persona. "Is there anything I can do for you?"

What was that about? Did he think he'd hook her up with some social services? Direct her to a food bank? Help her find a job with a great health plan?

"No. I'm sorry." She ran a hand over the gleaming surface of the sideboard, whisking away nonexistent dust. "You…well, you reminded me of someone and it sort of hit me hard."

"Oh." For once, he had no rejoinder to that, no dispensation of advice. "Do you want me to go?"

She reached out and put a hand on his arm. "No. Not at all."

Her touch on him was sweet, soft. Every instinct in his body told him to back away, head out the door and go on his way, hitchhiking if need be. But there was something about her touch that reminded Noah, too, of someone.

Himself. A long time ago.

"Listen, why don't you stay for dinner? That way, you'll have a meal in you before you hit the road again. It's after Labor Day, so a lot of the beach restaurants here are closed down. You'd have to go into Quincy proper to find anything."

He knew he should say no. Unfortunately his mouth didn't take good direction from his brain. "Dinner sounds like a good idea."

He'd stay for dinner, but only because the feel of her hand on his arm had awakened nerves he'd thought had been severed by his years on the job. Because it felt nice to be a man for a minute, a man who didn't have the weight of other people's lives sitting on his conscience.

"Great! I'll set another place at the table." That smile spread across her face again, socking him in the gut—

And warning him that he'd just done the very thing he didn't want to do. Laid the first brick of a foundation with another person.

"Him? He's a sweetie-pie." As if living up to what she'd said, Charlie dropped to his back and offered up his belly for the personal treatment. His tail beat ferociously against the linoleum floor, keeping up a steady tempo of "you-like-me."

She let her fingers trail along his nape, then his ears, toying with the velvet tips. Charlie let out a groan and wriggled even closer.

"Now you've gone and done it," Noah said, laughing.

She jerked up to look at him. "Done what?"

"Spoiled him. Now he's going to make me get out the silk bed again."

She arched a brow. "Silk bed?"

"Charlie is the king of my mom's castle. He has his every whim indulged, sleeps on better sheets than Elvis did and even has his own teddy bear. She's only been gone twenty-four hours and already called me three times to make sure I'm treating him right."

"And are you?"

"Well, I drew the line at the silk bed and the Burberry trench coat."

Victoria chuckled. "He's a nice dog, though. I can see why she spoils him."

Noah wasn't so bad himself. Though "nice" might not be the first word that Victoria would use when asked to describe him. Gorgeous, with a haunting quality that told her a lot of him was kept behind a locked door.

Silence hummed between them and once again, Victoria wanted to kick herself. She was a complete and total social moron. She'd spent too much time here in this house, away from the real world. Away from other people.

But that was going to change.

She scrambled for something to say, something to fill the uncomfortable gap between them, to help her stop noticing the deep color of his eyes, the way one lock of dark hair stubbornly fell against his forehead. Strong, sexy and most of all, unaware of the effect he could have on a woman.

Focus, she told herself. Focus.

"I almost forgot about the mechanic. Larry is the guy we use. Used," she corrected herself, since the car hadn't needed service in a long time because she had yet to muster the courage to get behind the wheel again. She'd learned to drive years ago, but had never driven outside of Quincy. The thought of taking the car on the highway—or into the city—was way too much. "Anyway, his number is on the corkboard beside the phone."

"Thanks." Noah crossed the kitchen, found the name Larry on the neat, alphabetized list of names and numbers and dialed. When the phone was answered on the other end, Noah explained he was looking for Larry and needed a tow as well as a few repairs. "That'll do. Thanks," he said finally, then hung up the phone.

"Is Larry on his way?" Victoria asked, pretending she didn't care, that the thought of company to help while away the long evening that stretched before her wasn't as tempting as a bucket of chocolate.

"Yep. Be here in half an hour." As he said the words, his stomach rumbled. "Listen, if my being here is difficult for you, we can forget dinner. I'll get out of your hair." He looked down at the dog, who had taken a proprietary space between Victoria's feet. "We'll both get out of your hair soon as the tow truck arrives."

"You can't leave," she said, grinning. "Or I'll end up eating leftover pot roast three times a day for a week."

"Pot roast? I haven't had that in about a hundred years."

"Sorry it's nothing more fancy. The roast happened to be what I had in the freezer. When I put it in the Crock-Pot, I knew I'd have way too many leftovers since it's only me here, but—" She laughed. "Can you tell I haven't had any company in a while? My mother used to say once my motor was running, there was no turning it off."

Noah laughed. "I have a brother like that. Talks a blue streak sometimes about absolutely nothing. He—"

The words cut off as abruptly as they came. Victoria wanted to ask, to press him for more, but wouldn't. She liked her privacy. She certainly couldn't fault him for wanting the same.

And yet, in his eyes, she saw defeat, weariness. The emotions were too powerful, too private, and her gaze went to the floor, as if studying the black-and-white squares would provide some answer from the cosmos. They didn't. What did she expect from forty-year-old linoleum anyway? "So, how do you like your roast?"

He grinned, clearly glad for the change of subject. "Done mooing."

She laughed. "Do you like your potatoes baked? Or cooked with the meat?"

"Are you making gravy?"

"Of course." Charlie started running excited circles around them, as if he understood the conversation.

"Then in with the meat."

"Biscuits?"

"Homemade?" he asked, clearly teasing. Maybe even…flirting?

"Is there any other kind?" she said, returning the smile, the vibrations in the air.

"Not in my book." His smile turned into a wide grin that seemed to take over his features and cast them in an entirely different light.

A sexy light.

The kind that lit a fire within Victoria's belly that had never really been lit before. She swallowed, suddenly very glad she'd paid attention when her mother taught her to cook. "Carrots?" she said, the word a squeak.

"The whole works," Noah replied, his gaze on hers.

The whole works. Well, heck, then she was going to bake a pie. Maybe even find that lone bottle of wine she'd been saving for a special occasion.

"I'm looking forward to it," Noah said. "It's been a hell of a long time since I had a home-cooked meal."

Something about the way he'd said the words, the pained look that filled his green eyes, the way his shoulders seemed to drop...it all made her want to ask. To probe.

To help.

Because if there was one thing Victoria Blackstone did well, it was help other people. Florence Nightingale reincarnated, that was her.

She drew back, though. Helping Noah, getting involved with Noah, would detract from the plan. Tomorrow, there was going to be a whole new Victoria on the block.

But for tonight, there was Noah, his dog and a dinner to get on the table.

Because if there were ever two people she'd seen

who deserved the whole works, at least for one meal, it was herself and this mysterious stranger.

An hour later, Noah sat at Victoria's dining room table, Charlie lying at his feet, hoping to get lucky with a stray crumb, despite having devoured his own plate of meat. Noah had been as quick as the dog in downing his first helping of pot roast and was now making big dents in his second. The food was delicious, and had filled the permanently hungry ache in a belly that had subsisted for too long on fast food. "I haven't had a homemade meal in years," he said, wiping his mouth with a crisp white cloth napkin.

"Really?"

"I'm a bachelor. I can order take-out, and open a can of dog food."

"For you or the dog?" She grinned and tipped her wine toward him.

He chuckled. "Based on the kind of fast-food junk I feed myself, I'd say Charlie gets the better end of the deal."

Her laughter was soft and easy, a sound that seemed centuries away from the stiff, uncomfortable furniture filling her house. And a million miles away from the contemporary, stark loft Noah had just left.

He looked around at the floral wallpaper, his gaze sweeping over the brown shag living room carpet butting against the wood floor in the doorway, and thought maybe it was closer to two million miles.

"Go ahead, ask," Victoria said.

"Ask what?"

"Why my house looks like something you'd see on *TV Land*. I can tell you're wondering."

"Oh, no, I…" His voice trailed off, no ready excuse to fill the space.

"My parents," Victoria said, laying her fork across her plate, "didn't like change. They took great pride in sleeping in the same bed all their lives, using the same stove for twenty-five years, making good use of the carpet that came with the house and grudgingly replaced a couple of rooms when the old carpet wore out. Call it frugal, sentimental…I'm not sure. But they liked things to stay exactly the same, day after day."

"Liked?" he asked, catching the past tense. "You lost your mother, too?"

She nodded and started working on the interstate highway system in her potatoes again, but didn't eat. "A couple months before my father. I've been here alone ever since. And well—" at this, she let out a sigh and looked around the dated room "—I haven't had the heart to change anything." She paused, took a second look and added, "Yet."

Curiosity nudged at Noah. He wanted to know more, like what she meant by "yet." And why she seemed to hold back parts of herself as she spoke, as if she was filtering out the bad scenes of her story.

Noah knew those signs. Knew the way someone sounded when they tried to paint a pretty picture, instead of telling him the truth, the whole truth and nothing but the truth.

So help him God.

But in the end, he hadn't been all that good at divining the truth, had he? He may have seen the signs, but he'd ignored them, all the way down to the bottom. And in doing so, he'd disappointed the one person who was depending on him to make things right—his brother.

And now, Justin was on the streets, out of Noah's grasp.

Against his hip, his now recharged cell phone began to vibrate. He glanced down at the number, then muted the ringer. He couldn't deal with that.

Not now anyway.

What could he say to Robert, who was fighting a war on the other side of the world? "Oh, yeah, I know I screwed up when I promised I'd rescue your kid. But don't worry. The same system that failed him will surely save him."

He'd be throwing platitudes at a disaster, like using a squirt bottle to put out a five-alarm fire.

"There's an apple pie, too," Victoria said, interrupting his thoughts. "I baked it while you were outside helping Larry get your truck loaded up."

"I had an aunt," Noah said, the memory slipping from his lips before he could stop it, "who used to make us all fruitcakes for Christmas. The trouble was, she didn't know how to bake. She was pretty nearsighted and had a little trouble telling the teaspoons from the tablespoons."

Victoria laughed. "Oh, I shouldn't laugh, but I can just imagine how badly that went."

"Hey, at least you didn't have to eat it."

"I promise, mine will be better."

Noah's stomach growled with a memory of the dozens of pies of his childhood, served warm, cold, however, but always good. The sweet scent in the air formed a mental image with the treat baking in Victoria's oven. "It's been a really long time since I've had pie."

"Pies are like families, don't you think?" she asked, raising a fork to make her point. "No crust is exactly the same, but all the ingredients in the filling make it turn out perfect."

"Not all families are like that," he said quietly. "Not by a long shot."

Victoria opened her mouth to say something, surely to ask him what he'd meant by that. He stood and tossed his napkin onto the table, the now silent cell phone a heavy reminder of the reality he was avoiding. "I'm, ah, full. Rain check on the pie?"

"Sure." But the look of disappointment in her eyes made him feel awful.

She didn't understand and he couldn't explain.

Noah gathered up his dishes and headed into the kitchen. Charlie trailed after him, but wisely kept his own counsel about his temporary owner and curled up in a corner, leaving Noah's jeans unscathed. Noah loaded the dishes in the sink, ran some water and squirted some soap over them, then turned and looked around the kitchen. No dishwasher.

Somehow, it didn't surprise him. He began to wash, circling his plate over and over again, trying to scrub off a crimson stain that didn't exist. One that wouldn't disappear, no matter how many times he blinked.

"Are you okay?" Victoria's quiet voice at his shoulder.

"Yeah." *No.* He hadn't been okay in a long damned time.

"It's clean," she said, gently taking it from his hands, running it under the water and putting it into the dish drainer. The action brought her closer to him, her breasts brushing against his back, the sweet fruit scent she wore whispering around them. She was warmth and goodness, something he hadn't thought existed, at least not in his corner of the world.

He inhaled her fragrance. *Kiss her. Kiss the woman who made you a pot roast. Baked you a pie.*

Cared.

No. A kiss would only extend the thread between them, adding another knot in the tenuous string already begun.

He reached into the sink, picked up his glass and plunged the sponge into it, again and again, seeing all his mistakes pile up in the soap bubbles, quadrupling onto each other, weighing on him like so many stones.

"Noah." She laid a hand on his shoulder. The touch suddenly seemed too much.

"Don't," he said, his voice a growl, a warning. "Don't get close to me."

She backed up, and he immediately wished he could take the words back, hit Rewind, do it again with more tact and less anger. But she'd gotten between him and some mighty bad damned memories. Victoria had just become another casualty in the war with himself.

And that wasn't fair.

He spun around, the water dripping from his hands onto the checkerboard tile. "I'm sorry. I—"

What could he tell her? That he'd let down the only people in the world he loved? The only family he really had?

That he'd failed with the one kid who'd needed him more than any other? That he hadn't been able to say the right words or be there at the right time to stop a life from spiraling into the depths? That he'd kept the real truth about Justin's street life from Robert, because

Noah had thought he, of all the people in the fourteen-year-old's life, had the right combination to pull him back from the brink?

That he was a man who deserved to be alone, to hide from the world and lick his wounds?

Way to make a good first impression, McCarty.

"I know," she said, and she approached him again, clearly not afraid of his grizzly bear attitude. She reached out. He watched her hand approach, telling himself he should back away, run from her.

From contact. From caring.

But then her hand touched his arm, warm skin against warm skin, and the human part of Noah that he had told himself was dead roared to life, craving the touch, the nearness of someone who had that understanding look in her eyes.

Longing. Needing. So very desperately needing this, just for now, just this once.

"Noah," she said again, his name slipping from her tongue as gently as the summer breeze.

He swallowed hard. Then he ignored the warning bells in his head, leaned forward and kissed her.

CHAPTER THREE

WHEN Noah McCarty's lips met hers, Victoria's entire world screeched to a halt.

It wasn't that she'd never been kissed before—she had, several times—it was the *way* he kissed her. Like he'd discovered a buried treasure and was intent on preserving it instead of plundering it.

His lips drifted over hers, slow, sure. Tasting. Exploring. Igniting. The blood rushed to her head, thundering in her pulse, and everything below her neck melted into a helpless puddle of hormones. She had read about kisses like this, dreamed of receiving one, but never, ever imagined a man could truly do such wonderful things with such a small part of her anatomy.

And then, he brought his hands, still damp from the dishes, up to cup her face. That was the touch that sealed it for Victoria, that sent her already frenzied hormones over the edge, screaming for more of whatever Noah McCarty had.

At first, she didn't touch him back. Her lips returned the kiss, but her arms remained stubbornly at her side, as reclusive as she had been, afraid he was a mirage, a

That seemed as good a word as any, Noah figured. Although, guests didn't kiss the hostess. Guests were smart enough to eat the pie instead of thinking about devouring her lips.

Well, if that were true, then where had that kiss come from? Definitely out of left field. He'd merely been sideswiped by dinner, swept up into a moment he'd never intended.

Obviously Charlie hadn't been the only one overwhelmed by the roast beef.

"Mrs. Witherspoon," Victoria prompted, "did you come by for something?"

"Oh, yes. I did indeed. I'm putting in a greenhouse and I need to knock down a wall." She put a finger to her chin. "Maybe two. Can I borrow a sledgehammer?"

"Did you finish the patio already?"

Mrs. Witherspoon waved a hand in dismissal. "I'm going to turn that into a garden. Who needs all that space to sit around anyway?" She took a step forward, studying Noah. "How long are you staying, young man? And what are your intentions with our Victoria?"

Beside him, Noah could see Victoria cringe. He knew the look. He'd had a neighbor like Mrs. Witherspoon when he'd been a kid. Playing games at the knees of the local bridge club seemed to give them ownership when he got older, as if he were part of the extended family of every little old lady who had ever sipped tea at his mother's dining room table.

Or at least it used to be that way. Then his parents' marriage had run aground, and eventually, the neighbors had stopped calling, as if what had happened in the McCarty house was contagious. The weeds had taken over the front gardens and the friendly waves had been replaced by distant stares.

But now Mrs. Witherspoon was looking at him expectantly. "Uh, just until tomorrow," Noah said. "My truck broke down and Larry—"

"You're staying here? With Victoria?" Her shocked face told him what she thought of that. Apparently social mores hadn't changed since Noah had been a kid.

"He's renting my vacant room," Victoria cut in.

Mrs. Witherspoon harrumphed, removing her enormous hat and using a free hand to smooth her gray hair. "I had a man ask to rent one of my rooms once. He didn't want the extra twin, let me tell you." She pursed her lips and eyed Noah. "You come with me, young man. I'll put you to work knocking down a wall." She thought again. "Probably two."

"I'd love to help, ma'am, but I'm heading to Maine in the morning."

"Maine? Whatever for? I'll tell you something—" at this, she wagged her feathered hat "—there's nothing in Maine you can't find right here."

"Well—"

"Besides, this won't take much time. It's always good to keep busy, don't you think?"

"Well—"

"Now, go on, get that sledgehammer," Mrs. Witherspoon said, waving Noah in the direction of the garage, "while Victoria and I have a little chitchat. Then I suppose you can come back here and stay with our Victoria." She eyed him suspiciously. "After I give her some advice about handling strangers, of course."

For a second, Noah thought of protesting, then

changed his mind. Mrs. Witherspoon was right about one thing. Knocking down a wall would be good for him. For one, it would give him something to do, something to fill the hours until morning—something other than kissing Victoria again—and for another, it would help him work out a little of the tension building in his shoulders, bunching his muscles like coiled wire.

But an hour and a half and two walls later, Noah hadn't found relief in the destruction of plaster and lathe. He was sweaty and dusty, his body aching, his chest heaving, but the demons that had traveled with him from Rhode Island were still hanging stubbornly on his shoulders.

"Noah?"

Victoria's soft voice behind him. He turned, laying the sledgehammer against one of the remaining studs, swiping off the bead of sweat along his brow. "Hey."

"I brought you more lemonade. And, you have a call." She held up his cell phone, which he had left behind when he'd come over to Mrs. Witherspoon's. He hadn't thought to tell Victoria not to answer it. He hadn't thought to turn it off. He hadn't thought at all.

He stared at the Motorola, as if it might bite him. The small silver phone looked innocuous enough, but Noah knew better. Whoever was waiting on the other end would have questions. Questions Noah didn't know how to begin to answer.

"He said he's your boss," Victoria said, "and he told me to tell you that if you think you can get away without answering the phone, he has ways of making sure you hear him."

At that, Dan Higgins let out a roar through the cell line. "McCarty, pick up! I can hear you breathing, damn it!"

Despite himself, Noah grinned. Dan always did know how to motivate his employees.

Since there would be no getting rid of Dan, Noah crossed to Victoria and took the phone, then the lemonade. "Thanks."

She gave him a shy smile. "No problem."

As he swallowed a big gulp of the icy beverage, he told himself not to be touched that she'd gone to the trouble to make it. He'd seen her empty the pitcher earlier, which meant she'd had to make another one. Once again, lemon slices tangoed with the ice cubes, telling Noah this wasn't some store-bought mix he was drinking.

"I hear ice cubes," Dan shouted. "So don't play dead, McCarty. Talk to me."

"I'm here," Noah said. Reluctantly.

"Good. Now, you may think you quit, but you didn't."

"Which of those two words didn't you hear when I walked out this morning? I'm done, Dan. D-O-N—"

"You're on vacation. Leave. What do you call it…hiatus. Whatever. You'll be back."

Across from him, concern filled Victoria's face. Noah turned away, toward the expanse of Mrs. Witherspoon's yard that had once been blocked by a wall. He closed his eyes and gripped the icy glass tighter.

"Dan, I'm not coming back." He couldn't face another failure, not one where people's lives were at stake.

"Justin wasn't your fault," Dan said softly. "Sometimes—"

"Don't say it," Noah said, the words a growl. "He was my responsibility and I let him down. Now he's probably on the streets selling his soul for drugs, or, God

Almighty, something worse. And all because I didn't do my damned job."

"If you come back—"

"If I come back, all I'll end up seeing is Justin's face on a rap sheet. Or on a slab in the morgue. I can't do that, Dan. I can't—" Noah's voice broke on the last few words, splintering and cracking into shards sharper than those of the old wood that littered the ground at his feet. "I *quit*."

"Take all the time you need," Dan said, not giving up on him, refusing once again to hear what Noah said. "I'll be here, if you need me. I'll keep looking for him here, be his shadow for a while. Till you get back. If I hear anything about him, I'll call."

"Don't," Noah said, but the protest was a weak one. Good or bad, he still wanted to know, damn it all. He still cared.

That was the one part he couldn't hammer out of him no matter how hard he tried.

As he clicked off the phone, he felt a soft hand on his shoulder, smelled the sweet scent of apples. Victoria.

"Noah," she said quietly, her hand a caress against his tired muscles. "When you're done, the room is ready. If you still want it. And the pie is waiting, too." Then she turned and walked away, leaving him to make up his own mind.

For a man trying to be a hermit, he seemed to be overrun with people trying to get close to him. Which was exactly why he couldn't stay with Victoria Blackstone.

CHAPTER FOUR

CHARLIE was as easy to please as a four-year-old at Christmas. He trotted jauntily into the spare bedroom on the second floor, chose a corner on the green shag carpet, curled himself into a ball and went to sleep. As innocent and sweet as a cherub on Valentine's Day.

Victoria laughed. "Doesn't take much to make him happy."

He echoed her laughter. He was doing a lot of that lately. "That's not what my mother would say. To her, Charlie isn't happy if the heated mattress in his bed isn't set at precisely the right temperature or if he's not surrounded by a thousand dollars worth of toys. She'd never believe he slept on shag."

Noah lifted his duffel onto the double bed, laying it on the white chenille spread. The furniture was maple, with little adornment. Simple, functional and as old as the rest of the house. "This is nice."

"Thanks." Victoria pivoted, as if seeing the room for the first time. "I painted the walls, changed the curtains, but haven't done much else to the space."

She'd chosen a soft mint that Noah was surprised to

find he liked. Sheer white curtains hung over the two double windows and drifted slowly in the breeze. Coupled with the white bedding, it gave the room a clean, comfortable look. The kind of place he'd seen in magazines.

"Considering my decorating skills, this is the Taj Mahal." He grinned. "My apartment is done in Early Bachelor."

She leaned against the doorjamb, arms over her chest. She raised a knowing brow. "Meaning you have a recliner, a TV and a fridge full of beer?"

He chuckled. "Yeah, all the comforts of a single man's life."

Although, if Noah were being honest, comfort and his life in the past few years hadn't exactly gone together. Standing in this room, he felt for a second like maybe he could change that.

And maybe he'd be better off just holing up in Mike's cabin and letting his beard grow to his knees.

Noah crossed to the window. The sun was making its journey down to the horizon, streaks of orange glinting off the rippling ocean waters, like prisms on a chandelier. He stood in awe at the miraculous beauty of Nature. "I don't think I've watched a sunset in years."

"If that's the case, then we need to watch it from outside," Victoria said, grabbing his hand and tugging him from the room. "Come on, or we'll miss it."

Before he knew it, they'd gone down the stairs and out the back door, onto a covered porch that faced the ocean. A small patch of grass led to the beach, and then to the ocean quietly lapping at the land.

Her hand in his was warm, perfect. Neither of them

let go, maybe because it felt right, in keeping with the majestic view ahead.

"Take off your shoes," Victoria said.

"Take off my—"

She grinned. "You want the full experience? Then trust me."

Trust her. Trust a woman he'd met a few hours ago, a woman who had obviously done that with him, by opening her house without hesitation. She'd let him in, instantly believing the best about him.

When was the last time he had looked at anyone and seen nothing but the best? When had he last thought that he could trust someone, without reservation? So many bricks, too many, had been shorn up against his heart.

Victoria had already slipped off her flats and looked as comfortable in the sand as the terns that darted along the edge of the shore.

Noah bent over, loosened the laces of his boots, then took them and his socks off. The instant his feet hit the cool sand, relaxation seeped into his pores.

"Let's go down to the water's edge," she said, taking his hand again and leading him forward, all the way to where the ocean was inching forward, one wave at a time, onto the damp sand.

Cold water hit his feet, a surprise considering the still-warm air. The water was about sixty degrees, far too cold to go swimming, but not too cold to stand along the edge, toes squishing into the thick, wet sand.

"Isn't it beautiful?"

Ahead of them was, indeed, true beauty. The sun had lowered itself to what looked like the edge of the world, oranges and yellows diffusing across the sky, puddling into the ocean. The two of them stood there for several long, silent moments, watching Nature's splendor go to bed. It all looked so peaceful, so quiet, and so unlike the congestion and noise of Providence.

"Do you see that dark lump in the water?" Victoria said. "That's Seal Rock. Past it, you can see the city skyline. It's quite an amazing sight at night, isn't it? Almost…magical."

And it was, he thought, as the lights of the city began to turn on, twinkling in the part of the day that seemed suspended between night and day. The water slipped around their feet, slowly deepening.

Noah turned, his gaze going to Victoria's lips, his entire mind caught up in the same twilight magic. He leaned forward, about to kiss her, pushing the consequences away, when he noticed a tan body darting off with stolen booty in his mouth.

Charlie.

And Noah's sock.

"Charlie!" But the dog didn't stop. Didn't even falter. Just kept going, running in a wild circle around the beach, the sock dragging from his tiny jaws like a prize rabbit.

Victoria laughed, then let go of Noah's hand and took off after the dog. Noah scrambled up the beach, cornering the dog from the other side, but neither of them managed to catch the wily Chihuahua. He escaped their grasp, again and again.

As she ran, laughter escaped from Victoria, the happy sound echoing across the empty beach. At first, Noah had only felt annoyance for the dog who clearly thought this thievery was a game. But then, Victoria's happiness caught him like a cold and a moment later, he heard the sound of his own laughter joining hers like a harmony to her melody.

He darted to the left, reached for Charlie, missed, then stumbled forward at the same time Victoria did. Slipping on the sand, they nearly collided, chests heaving, breath coming in bursts. He reached out a hand to steady her, forgetting the dog, the beach, everything but this woman.

He took a step forward, his gaze riveted on the teeming ocean in her eyes, the way her lips parted ever so slightly, as if she, too, was waiting.

Waiting for him to kiss her.

He brushed his lips against hers, intending a momentary touch, but then, found himself wrapping his arms around her, drawing Victoria's warmth to his chest, needing that touch more than he'd ever needed anything in his life. Beneath his mouth, her lips were sweet, tender, returning his kiss with a fervor that told him he wasn't the only one caught in the spell of the sunset.

At his feet, Charlie growled, shaking the sock back and forth against his bare ankle. Noah tried to ignore him, but when the dog started jumping up between them, using the sock like a white flag, it was impossible to stay serious about kissing Victoria.

They broke apart, both laughing at the same time. The shared humor, heightened by the darkness closing around them, took everything up a notch.

Or ten.

"That dog—" Noah began, about to curse Charlie's timing. As if hearing the growl in Noah's voice, Charlie took off and promptly started digging a hole to bury Noah's sock.

"This is the most fun I've had in a year." She laughed again.

Noah shook his head, giving up on the now buried treasure that had been on his foot a few minutes earlier, then chuckled. "You're right. It was fun."

She shivered, wrapping her arms around herself. Without the warmth of the sun, the ocean wind had dropped the temperature a few degrees. "Let's go inside. I'll let you get settled in, take a shower or just get some rest. Though after you spent all that time working for Mrs. Witherspoon, I wish I had a hot tub to offer you."

Hot tub. Victoria. Long night.

There was an image he didn't need. All it would do was get him in trouble. He wasn't here for anything more than a night's sleep.

Uh-huh. That's exactly why he was standing on a beach kissing her while the city lights winked knowingly.

Despite those intentions, the night stretched ahead of him, endless and empty, like so many nights before. There was no TV in the room where he was staying, which meant he'd be left with his own thoughts for the next few hours until exhaustion finally won the battle over his guilty conscience. Right now, that was the last kind of company Noah needed.

"Do you ah…play poker?" he asked, spitting out the first thing that came to mind. He couldn't have screamed typical bachelor more if he was wearing a frat symbol on his forehead.

"Poker?" Victoria grinned. "For pennies or toothpicks?"

"Considering I'm currently between employment opportunities, how about toothpicks?"

"You're on. I'll grab the cards while you unpack. Meet you in the kitchen." She headed into the house, with Noah bringing up the rear, leaving his footwear as Charlie's buried treasure.

A few minutes later, Noah found Victoria at the table, shuffling a deck of red Bicycle cards. Two rose-patterned teacups filled with toothpicks sat at either end of the table, ready and waiting.

He slid into the opposite seat and watched her expertly shuffle the cards, then slide the deck over to him. "Cut?" she said.

He grinned and did as she asked. Victoria deftly picked up the deck and dealt five cards to each of them. The woman knew how to play cards, that was evident. Another surprise to Noah. Just when he thought he had Victoria Blackstone pegged, she went and turned the tables.

"Were you a dealer in a previous life?" he asked.

She laughed. "No. My parents weren't much for going out and they loved poker, so…" She shrugged.

"They dealt in their five-year-old?"

"Basically, yeah." She gave him a grin that managed to seem both sexy and challenging. Something Noah had thought was long dead stirred in his gut.

She wagged a finger at him. "I warn you, I'm good."

"Glad I'm only betting toothpicks." He reached into the teacup. "What's the ante?"

"Let's make it five."

"Ooh, a woman who lives dangerously." He tossed five of the thin wooden slivers into the center of the table, waited until she did the same, then picked up his cards. Two eights and a jumble of suits and numbers

go," she said, laying the pie in front of
aken the time to pop it into the microwave,
e dessert enough that the scoop of vanilla
ed on top was already puddling around the
e flaky crust.

d—and smelled—like home. Like the kind
he saw in coffee commercials where the
on returned for Christmas. Noah's hand hes-
r his fork.

tched as Victoria selected a sliver of the warm
The bite disappeared between her lips with
ecision, barely a glisten from the cinnamon
juices lingering on her glossy coral mouth.
ving rocketed through him. For the pie. For her.
ther one of those heart-stopping kisses. Every-
ithin him wanted to lean forward, to taste the
ade goodness on her mouth.

h Herculean effort, Noah pushed those thoughts
He'd already been drawn in too much, gotten too
He dug into his pie and wasn't surprised to find
bite better than the last. "You're a great cook."
e blushed and dipped her head, her fork toying
a crumble of crust. "Thanks."

oo bad you weren't running the roach coach."
e arched a brow. "Roach coach?"

ou know, the canteen truck that comes at lunch-
? Loaded with foods only edible by roaches. But we
going to it all the same, gluttons for punishment
we government workers are."

What's a canteen truck? I mean, I know what a
teen is, I've seen them on *M*A*S*H* and shows like
, but what's a canteen truck?"

made up the other three. He slid the odd cards over to
her. "Three please."

Her face became serious, clearly in game mode. She
dealt him his cards, then replaced one of her own.
"Dealer takes one."

"You're quite the card shark." Noah bit back a grin.
He picked up his new cards, then fanned out his replen-
ished quintet. Two eights, two threes and a ten. Nothing
to write home about, but not so bad, either. "I'll bet
three." He slid his toothpicks into the center.

"I'll see your three and raise you—" she paused,
looking at her teacup "—three more."

"Call." He may only be playing with toothpicks, but
he wasn't going to bet the farm on two average pairs.
He tossed in three more toothpicks then placed his cards
on the table, spreading them out. "Two couples. Eights
and threes."

A grin turned up one corner of her mouth. "Sorry,
Noah, but I have three ladies here who'd like to meet
you." She laid down a triplet of queens.

Victoria gave him a smile of triumph. It radiated
through her face, arching her cheekbones and sparking
in her eyes. It was playful and serious all at once,
making Noah wonder what other juxtapositions this
woman had besides the time-warp house and the poker
expertise.

"You must be hell at the Texas Hold 'Em competi-
tions," Noah said.

"Actually I haven't played in years. Not since…"
Her voice trailed off, the smile disappearing. Then she
forced a brightness back into her face. "Anyway, not for
a long time."

Noah refused to wonder about that temporary glitch of sadness on her face. It wasn't his job anymore to worry about people and he wasn't staying here long enough to start.

All he wanted was to be king of the toothpick mountain. "Neither have I. Not since college anyway." He tossed his losing hand onto the deck of cards. "Apparently I haven't lost my touch for losing."

She laughed, then slid the deck over to him to deal. "Do you want to quit now or try to win back your toothpicks?"

If there was one thing he couldn't resist, it was a challenge. "Double or nothing," Noah said, then started shuffling.

An hour later, Noah was down to two toothpicks and Victoria's triumphant smile had taken permanent residence on her lips. He'd been bested by his temporary landlord. "That explains why I never had any money when I was in college," he said.

"I was just lucky." She raked up the cards, stacked them into a neat pile. "Do you want to play something else? Gin? Rummy?"

He glanced again at his dismal toothpick stash. So much for his goal of being king of the toothpick pile. Right now he wasn't even a page in the king's court. "I think I'm more the Go Fish kind."

She laughed. "Go Fish it is. But first, let me get us some of that pie and a glass of white wine." She smiled at him, this time a softer look that seemed, in an odd way, to thank him. "This is fun. I haven't had such a good time in ages."

Neither had he. When had he stopped having fun? In college, he'd had his share of parties and freshman

pranks. Though fun wa[...]
days of loud music and [...]

After he graduated, he [...]
college and high school [...]
off for a beer and a chanc[...]
Bruins on Friday nights. Th[...]
over more and more of hi[...]
moved on, to other cities, oth[...]
That left Noah with his cat, [...]
the hockey team won, as long [...]
of tuna on the counter. With th[...]
with Charlie, who preferred to [...]
on the legs of his furniture.

Talk about a pathetic way to s[...]

As Victoria started dishing up [...]
of her room for rent, of his quest f[...]
live. What was so wrong with stay[...]

For a little while, he told himse[...]
couple of days, a week at the most, j[...]
win back his toothpicks.

Uh-huh. That was all he wanted. A [...]
flushes and a bit more pot roast.

He watched Victoria slice two thick[...]
pie, the outline of her hourglass figure [...]
view. The woman was so obviously [...]
those who liked to set up house, care f[...]

Noah didn't need a nester. If anythin[...]
temporary fling, the kind that left him w[...]
guilt or expectations.

A woman like Victoria, he already knew, [...]
She was the kind men married, had kids w[...]
a house with, in cozy country style or some[...]

"Here yo[...]
him. She'd [...]
warming th[...]
she'd drop[...]
edges of th[...]

It look[...]
of home [...]
prodigal s[...]
itated ove[...]

He wa[...]
dessert. [...]
quick p[...]
flavored[...]

A cr[...]

For an[...]
thing [...]
homem[...]

Wit[...]
aside.[...]
close.[...]
every[...]

Sh[...]
with [...]

"[...]
S[...]
"[...]

time[...]
kee[...]
that[...]

can[...]
tha[...]

"Didn't they have one where you work?"

"I…" She studied the pie again. "I don't work."

"Well, wherever you used to work."

She shrugged. "I never have."

"What, worked? Everyone's had a job."

"Not me."

He blinked. "Not even a paper route?"

"Nope. Something always got in the way."

Victoria was in her late twenties, at the very most, thirty, Noah estimated. Definitely old enough to have worked at something. He'd never known a single person who hadn't at least had a paper route, a stint at McDonald's. Some kind of job.

He could tell, by looking at the house and watching the way she frugally stored all the leftovers, using exactly the right amount of plastic wrap, that she wasn't independently wealthy. There didn't seem to be a sugar daddy around, and she couldn't be making that much off of renting a single room. How on earth did she make ends meet?

He told himself not to worry. That this woman, and everything about her, wasn't his concern.

"If it had worked out where you could have had a job," he asked, "what would you have done?"

She stood and moved to the sink, depositing her plate, with Noah following. She shrugged. "I don't have a degree, so I really never considered a whole lot of options."

He waved a hand like a magic wand. "Pretend you already have one. What would you do?"

"If I could be anything…" Victoria began, her voice trailing off in thought. "Well, I don't know what I'd be." She laughed.

"You've never thought about it?"

"Oh, I have, but to suddenly have all those possibilities ahead, it seems so vast, so big of a choice. How will I know what I'm going to be happy doing for the rest of my life? Or if it's even what I'm meant to be doing in the greater scheme of things?"

He certainly wasn't the one to ask about that. He'd thought he'd picked a job where he could be happy but clearly, he'd been wrong. "I used to feel that way," he said. "Before I started working in the juvenile justice system as a probation officer, I used to think my job choice could change the world."

"I bet you did," she said softly, laying a hand on his arm. "One kid at a time."

He shook his head. "Maybe for a few of them, but certainly not for all."

She smiled. "Even God doesn't expect perfection."

Was that what Noah was doing? Expecting perfection from himself? From the kids he worked with? "Maybe you're right. But I've had a hard time seeing even one child slip through the cracks." He heaved a sigh, thinking of all the children who had refused the help they so desperately needed.

"You threw them the lifelines they needed, Noah. All they had to do was grab one and climb on out."

"Too many never did."

"And are those the ones that you're trying to outrun by going to Maine?"

Once again, Victoria had nailed him, finding the exact reasons for his actions. He turned away, not wanting to answer that question, to answer the questions it raised in himself. Noah reached for the faucet, turning on the water and avoiding the subject with a little Ivory dish soap.

Before he could grasp the sponge, Victoria raised herself on her tiptoes and place a quick, chaste kiss on his cheek. "You're a good man, Noah McCarty," she whispered in his ear, just before withdrawing.

He wasn't, but she couldn't know that. Just for tonight, he'd let Victoria—and himself—believe those words.

Outside the small kitchen window, night was in full swing. The moon and the city sparkled diamond chips of light on the water. The ocean breeze whispered through the open window. Noah inhaled, suddenly realizing how long it had been since he'd had time to smell the roses. Or whatever it was that a guy took the time to smell.

A woman's perfume? Particularly one made up of citrus and sweet, something as fresh and innocent as a new dawn?

"Let's, ah, get these dishes done," he said, changing the subject.

Beside him, Victoria started to hum, an old Burt Bacharach tune he recognized from his childhood. For a second, Noah allowed himself to be wrapped up in the spell of domesticity. Him washing, her drying, a comfortable silence descending between them, broken only by the sweet melody of her voice. He handed her the last plate, then pulled the plug on the sink. "That's it."

"Thanks." She offered him a teasing grin. "Do you want to try for a rematch?"

Against his hip, his cell phone began to vibrate. Noah unclipped it and looked at the number displayed on the caller ID. His brother, calling from Iraq. Undoubtedly seeking answers, answers Noah didn't have. But most of all, looking for hope.

Noah had run out of that a long time ago.

"Thanks for the pie," he said, the reality of the phone reminding him that he wasn't what she thought. "But I better get to bed. Still have a long drive ahead of me tomorrow if the truck is ready."

Then he left the room, heading out into the hall to answer the cell. Robert was somewhere on the other side of the world, in the middle of his second tour of duty with the Army, the static across the line clear evidence of the miles separating them.

The conversation had been tense and short, like every conversation with his younger brother in the last fifteen years. Ever since Noah had left home and Robert had stayed behind, being the grown-up one. Robert had done that all his life, even raising Justin alone after his wife had taken off, making it clear she had no interest in raising a child or feigning domesticity.

He and Noah hadn't talked much over the years, not until Robert had been called up to Iraq and he'd asked Noah to become Justin's legal guardian, relying on Noah because his older brother was the expert at helping a troubled child.

The one to trust.

But after Noah hung up the phone, he felt like he'd only made Robert's misery worse. No, he didn't know where Justin was. No, he hadn't heard from him. Yes, he was sure the boy would be back.

He wasn't sure at all. He'd just tossed those words out, knowing that if he didn't believe them, he couldn't expect his brother to.

His thoughts went back to Victoria, to the words she'd whispered in his ear earlier. "You're a good man, Noah McCarty."

How he wished he could live up to that sentence. To be the kind of man who could stay here, with Victoria, chasing Charlie around the beach, eating pie and building a life, a family of his own.

Hell, he couldn't even take care of the little family he had now—not to mention one three-pound dog. He had no business even thinking about building a family with someone else.

Soon as morning broke, he was out of here. Whether Charlie liked the carpet or not.

CHAPTER FIVE

SLEEP refused to come.

Around two, Noah threw off the covers, slipped out of bed, pulled on a pair of sweats and padded barefoot down the stairs and into the dark kitchen. Seeking what, he didn't know. Anything that would quiet his thoughts and give him at least one night of rest.

He didn't find Mr. Sandman in the refrigerator or any of the pantry cupboards. At least, not until he reached the last one, high above the refrigerator. There, Mr. Sandman was having a party with his good friend Captain Morgan and his other best friend, Jack Daniel's. Their faces smiled back at him in invitation, promising a good time. Noah took a long, long look at the bottles, then shut the door.

All Captain Morgan and Jack Daniel's could offer was temporary relief, followed by a compounding of reality the next morning. Noah had seen enough lives ruined by alcohol to want to do it to himself.

With a sigh, he sat down in one of the kitchen chairs. The smooth linoleum was cool against his feet. He toyed with the salt and pepper shakers on the table, a matched pair of mini Kewpie dolls that looked like something won at a state fair.

"Couldn't sleep?"

He turned around, startled by the sound of Victoria's voice. "Yeah. Same with you?"

She shrugged. "I don't sleep much. Ever."

He chuckled. "Me, neither."

"Do you want a snack?" When he nodded, she headed to the refrigerator. Noah remained rooted to the chair, watching her.

In all his life, he couldn't remember seeing a woman who dressed like her, who seemed so…homey and yet with a decidedly sexy flair. Beneath a short, thin white robe, she wore a soft pink nightgown, trimmed with delicate scalloped lace. The diaphanous material drifted around her calves, angel-like. Her feet were bare, tipped with coral painted toes. As she moved through the kitchen and opened the refrigerator door, the incandescent light shone against the sheer fabric.

And nearly right through it. Oh-boy.

Noah could see every curve, every valley, of her body. Something within him that had long been pushed aside began to stir, reminding him that he was a man—a man who had been alone far too long—and she was most definitely a woman. They were alone, no one else in this house but Charlie, who wouldn't have budged from his square of carpet for all the Milk-Bones in the world.

"Ham and cheese okay?" Victoria turned, a package of deli meat in her hand.

Noah barely registered the food. All he saw was the golden light around her and the way it gave him X-ray vision into exactly what Victoria Blackstone looked like when she went to bed. And what she'd look like if she went to bed with him.

"Noah?"

"Uh…sure." He shook his head, ridding it of thoughts that would do nothing but get him into trouble. "Sure."

She laughed. "You must be really hungry. You answered me twice."

"Ravenous." But what he wanted right now couldn't be found at the local deli. That was for damned sure.

She loaded the sandwich fixings into her arms and shut the refrigerator door, snuffing out the light. Damn.

Victoria moved to the counter, where a square of moonlight bounced off a breadboard. She began making the sandwiches, deftly applying the mayonnaise to four slices of hearty oat bread, then layering on the meat and cheese, topping it off with slices of tomato and lettuce. It was a sandwich that made his mouth water. She cut each neatly on the diagonal, loaded them onto stoneware plates, then handed one to him.

"You sure know how to make a sandwich," he said. Noah took a bite, savored the flavor, then nodded approvingly. "A really good sandwich."

She chuckled. "Wonder if I could have a career in that."

He toyed with the edge of the plate, running his thumb along the floral circle. "Thank you," he said.

"For what?"

"For letting a perfect stranger—and his strange dog—into your house. For feeding us. For…" His voice trailed off, unable to release the last sentence, to thank her for saying what she had earlier that night. True or not, it had given him a much-needed variation in his perspective, at least for a little while.

"It was my pleasure," she said, the soft smile crossing her features telling him that she meant it. "I have to admit, though, that I had an ulterior motive in feeding you."

He arched a brow. "Ulterior motive?"

"In the last few months, this house—" she looked around the darkened room "—has become like a prison. I used to love it here, used to think I could live in this house forever, but lately…"

"You want more."

She nodded. "But…" She heaved a sigh. "I'm afraid."

"You? Afraid? Afraid of what? You strike me as the strong, self-sufficient type."

"Oh, I am, as long as I'm here, within these walls. All that changes when I walk out the front door."

Another piece added to the Victoria puzzle. She was such a contrast—this woman, who to him, seemed made of steel, yet as vulnerable as a reed in the wind. "Why?" he probed.

"Because I've always been here. And I don't just mean in the traditional, this-is-where-I-grew-up sense. It went beyond that." She laced her hands together, laying them flat against the table, then went on. "I was homeschooled, which naturally kept me away from the rest of the kids. Even when they came home from school and played at the park, I was left out a lot. I mean, no one really knew me. My mother used to be a teacher and I know she thought she was doing the best for me, but it only increased my isolation."

"You never went to school?" His mind raked over the memories he had of elementary, middle and high school. The friends he'd made, the trouble he'd gotten into, the experiences that had helped shape him into the person he was today. He couldn't imagine not having gone through that—acne, bad dates and all.

She shook her head. "After a while, it was…convenient, I guess, for me to be home and not wrapped up in things like basketball practice and band concerts. And then, when I was thirteen, my father got ill and my mother needed help with him. Later, she got sick, so I stepped in as caretaker there, too."

He didn't say anything, just waited for her to continue, amazed by the story. She was the kind of woman who had lived the lives he saw every day, but had come out of it all on top, in his opinion.

"I was one of those late in life babies," she explained. "Very late. My parents didn't meet until they were in their thirties. My mother was forty-one when she had me. Neither of my parents had ever been very healthy. I guess the fitness craze passed over my house." She gave him a bittersweet smile.

"So you took care of them?"

She nodded. "It wasn't much at first, but by the time my dad retired from the shipyard, he was already pretty far gone. All that asbestos exposure had caught up with him. They didn't have all those rules about that stuff when he first started working, and I guess that's when all the damage was done."

Noah thought of his mother, alive and well and probably buying doggie toys in Europe. His father was still alive but as for where he was, Noah had no idea. Either way, he couldn't imagine doing what Victoria had done, putting her entire life on hold to care for her parents.

"My mother had a weak heart," she continued, the words tumbling from her faster with each sentence, as if she needed to get this story out, to tell someone, to share the words that he suspected had been kept within these walls for too long, "and I think seeing my dad decline was just too hard. She was juggling it all for so long—taking care of my father, doing some substitute teaching to help us make ends meet when he wasn't working anymore, teaching me, running the house. It was an awful lot on one woman's shoulders."

"What about you?" he asked gently. "Sounds like you had a lot on your shoulders, too."

She shrugged. "You don't think about it at the time. You just…do. It wasn't until both of them were gone that it hit me."

"What did?"

"I wasn't needed anymore." Her smile was watery, reflected in her eyes. "And it was my turn to move forward. I've just had a slow start, I guess."

Noah wasn't needed anymore, either, not since he'd walked out on his job. "I know what you mean," he said. "But sometimes moving forward is hard when you don't know which direction to go." It was the most he'd admitted to another person in his entire life, more than he'd admitted to himself in the last few days.

"Or if you've never moved in any direction," she added. "My parents were overprotective, and I'm just not used to being out and about."

"That can be a good thing. Believe me, with the kids I see, I wish more parents had an overprotective gene."

"Mine went a bit overboard." She popped a bite of ham in her mouth, swallowed, then went on. "When I was little, five, I think, the twelve-year-old girl across the street was abducted. It was one of those 'that could never happen in our neighborhood' kind of things. They never found her, and after a while, the family moved away."

"But the effects of that lingered, on everyone here," he said, the puzzle pieces beginning to fit, to square with the edges of this house and the way Victoria had lived.

"Yeah. I didn't even know her because she was older than me, but when that happened, it was enough for my parents to put up the glass walls around their only child."

His gaze strayed to the window. In the distance, the lights of Boston twinkled. How hard must that have been for her, living here all these years, looking out that window and seeing the city within reach and yet as distant as Jupiter.

"But," she said, her tone shifting into one of determination, optimism, "those days are over. I was hoping you could take me into the city tomorrow. I'll start there and tackle the rest of the world later." She grinned and newfound respect for her strength rolled through Noah. "We could be total tourists."

"Complete with the Red Sox caps and cameras?"

"That sounds perfect." She ate another piece of her sandwich, then looked up at him. "What's Providence like?"

He chuckled. "A lot like Boston, except without the beans and clam chowder."

She laughed. "Maybe I'll skip Providence then. I really want to go to Germany." She nodded when he arched a brow in surprise. "When I was a kid, I had this snow globe, you know, one of those musical kind where you shake it and the snow falls over the scene inside?"

"I had an aunt who collected them. You could get a regular blizzard going in her curio cabinet."

"My mother gave it to me for Christmas one year when I was, oh, maybe nine. Probably because I was always begging her to tell me stories with princesses in them."

"I was more the dragons and knight slaying type."

She laughed again. He marveled at how easily she laughed, how much she enjoyed the conversation—and how much he was enjoying it, too. "I loved that silly snow globe, because it had a castle in the center of the glass. On the bottom, it said the design was based on a real castle in Germany. In Heidelberg, or something like that. Anyway, I always dreamed of going there." A soft smile stole across her face. "Still do, I guess."

"I've seen a lot of this country," Noah said. "I haven't been outside of the U.S. yet, but I've been all over here. I've seen the best of people, the worst of people, the fanciest town houses and the dirtiest of slums."

"Did you like to travel?"

He thought back to when he first hit the road. In the quiet darkness that surrounded them, it felt right to let down his walls, an inch at a time. "It was exciting in the beginning, but then, it lost its flair. I always intended to travel again, but then work became the thing that kept me rooted to Providence. I always thought if I put in a few more hours, I could save another kid, turn one more life around."

"And so you, too, gave up an outside life for the people you cared about."

Victoria had just extended a bridge between them, connecting them in those ways that always seemed so serendipitous. She hadn't just sent a plank across the chasm between them, she'd built a whole bridge.

"And I walked away from it, too," he said, reminding her that he wasn't the saint she was depicting, not since he'd let Robert down.

He rose, putting physical distance between them, using the dirty plate as an excuse to cross the kitchen and leave those caring blue eyes behind him.

But Victoria, undaunted by his grizzly bear attitude, came up beside him, her warm hand soft on the cotton of his T-shirt, like a balm on an open wound. "What is it?"

"Nothing," he said, but the word came out like a growl.

"If you want to be alone..."

He spun around, capturing her hand with his, inhaling the sweet fragrance drifting off her skin. "No. I don't."

Hermit life be damned, right now, Noah McCarty didn't want to be alone at all.

Her gaze caught his, locked, held, then drifted down his face, lingering on his lips. Unbidden, his gaze went to her mouth, to the soft pink Cupid's bow waiting, expecting. Between them, the heat intensified, the temperature ratcheting up five, ten, fifteen degrees in an instant. Never had he been more aware of this slip of a woman, or the slip of nothingness she wore.

He swallowed hard, then reached forward, about to sweep her into his arms, to let her lips, her touch, her very presence, take away the demons in his mind.

For just one night.

But when her face turned up to meet his, all innocence and sweetness, Noah couldn't do it. He'd dragged himself down to the depths. He wasn't going to take Victoria with him.

If he went into Boston tomorrow with her, what would that accomplish? It would only fortify that bridge, adding cement to its foundations. Quadrupling his mistakes.

The city would cite me for an

laughed. "And the world would
"

She drew up her shoulders and
road ahead of her. "That's why I'm
today."

nto Boston? Alone?" Worry etched
therspoon's forehead.

ne." She grinned. "I haven't changed
ast twenty-four hours. I'm going with
hat's my plan."

ate, then." Mrs. Witherspoon beamed
ess, as if she'd just told Victoria so.
u're dressed so nicely."

she'd curled her hair, put on a skirt and
eater set didn't mean she was trying to
. She simply wanted to look nice. "No,
e. It's only a trip into the city," Victoria

nestly, Victoria, I see no other reason for
me with a man. Everything is all about
Eve."

kept her own counsel. Engaging Mrs.
on in a debate about love while there was
male a few feet away could only lead to
atchmaking. Victoria had her own goals—
didn't involve tying her life to someone else.
dless of what she'd considered doing with him
the moonlight last night.

Witherspoon leaned forward. "Just be careful,

The best thing he could do for her was to move on, to leave this woman who was so excited about the journey ahead, and hold his tongue when he wanted to tell her that sometimes, that journey was one you didn't want to make.

He released her and stepped back. "Thanks for the sandwich," he managed to say. "As for tomorrow, I really need to get on the road. Maybe Mrs. Witherspoon will want to do the tourist thing with you. I'm sorry." He walked out of the room, heading up the stairs and down the hall to his room before she could respond.

It was only after he shut the door and laid on top of the comfortable bed—a bed that would offer no sleep for him tonight—that Noah realized he'd done the very last thing he wanted to do.

Hurt Victoria.

CHAPTER SIX

EARLY Saturday morning, Victoria stood on the porch of the house where she'd spent her entire life and contemplated the road a few feet away, watching the tar turning from midnight-black to dark charcoal as the sun rose in the eastern sky. It was an ordinary road, filled with houses and the picturesque beauty of a remote, vacation-home suburbia, but it led to much more. To the city. To an area brimming with life, with options.

She had a car, she had gas. What she lacked was gumption.

However, what she did have sleeping in the back bedroom was a man. A man who surely wouldn't hyperventilate at the thought of going to the supermarket. A man who wouldn't find Boston traffic more terrifying than black widow spiders.

A man who unfortunately was planning on leaving today.

"Not if I have anything to say about it," Victoria said to herself. She was determined to change her life, starting today.

And starting with a man whose plans were about to

be
like
her

To
took fo

Not
in her k
been left
ing…or so

"What
Witherspoo
her reverie.
one hand, and
was, as always

"Enjoying th

"Nice day to
mused, sneaking a
path to the door. "To
She leaned forward,

"Fine."

Mrs. Witherspoo
answer. "I worry abou
this house for too long
were, are gone, and you
your own time."

She sighed. "It's hard,
committed, like I need to k
know it's crazy, but—"

"But it's what you feel," M
"What would happen if you
house, of the yard, of anyone e

She swallowed, recognizin

when she heard it.
overly tall lawn?"
Mrs. Witherspoo
not cave in, Victoria
"You're right."
glanced again at the
going into the city
"You're going
lines into Mrs. W
"Oh, no, not al
that much in the
Noah. At least, t
"Oh…on a d
with righteous
"That's why yo
Just because
a cashmere sw
impress Noah
no, not a dat
emphasized.
"Well, ho
spending ti
Adam and
Victoria
Witherspo
an eligibl
serious n
ones that
Rega
beneath
Mrs.

dear. I've never met a man who didn't have a few calluses. On his palms, or on his heart."

Victoria thought of Noah and decided he did, indeed, have a few calluses. His, however, all seemed to be on the inside. "I really haven't noticed his hands," Victoria lied. "Besides, I'm not looking for a man, Mrs. Witherspoon. Just a ride into the city."

"Uh-huh. A few laps around Government Center and next thing you know, you and he will have started a little world of your own. Before you know it, I'll be helping you hang mobiles and bunny wallpaper."

"I'm not..." Her voice trailed off as an unbidden image popped into her mind of Noah, bare-chested and cradling a baby.

Whoa. Brain overload.

Her only task today was to go into the city, not to think about settling down and making babies with Noah McCarty.

"If I had a man like him in my spare bedroom," Mrs. Witherspoon said, "I'd be thinking all that and more. Often."

"Mrs. Witherspoon, he's not interested in me like that. He's merely staying here until his truck is fixed."

"Oh, he's interested all right. I've seen the way he looks at you. You mark my words about that man," Mrs. Witherspoon said, pointing a gloved finger at Victoria and giving it a fateful shake. "You're going to end up with a lot more than some souvenir postcards."

Then she turned and walked away, the feathers on her hat bobbing in the breeze like dancing peacocks.

Victoria had no intentions of using Noah for anything more than a means to an end. She'd get him to take her into the city, to move past the end of the block, this little world she'd become so insulated within, and then let him go. On to Maine or wherever he was heading.

One step at a time—and none of them down a wedding aisle.

Last night, Noah had made it clear he was still as anxious to leave as a mallard duck delayed past the first frost. Something was bothering him, what, she didn't know. Either way, Victoria figured he needed a trip into the city as much as she did. A change of pace, of focus. A new beginning.

One she couldn't launch without him. There was no way she could drive into that city alone. Absolutely no way she could tackle the crowds, the noise, the congestion, without some backup.

And so, she was going to pull out the big guns—namely the ammunition in her cookbook.

First wave of attack: baked French toast with sliced apples.

Outside the shelter of the porch, a soft rain began to fall, nothing more than a heavy mist. The scent of the ocean hung heavy in the precipitation, as if the very sea were dropping onto her lawn.

A whimper sounded behind her. Victoria turned and saw the little Chihuahua sitting on the other side of the screen door, his nose sniffing the damp air, his tail down. "Oh, Charlie. It's not so bad. Come on out." She opened the door and let him through.

The tiny dog gave her a dubious look. He trotted forward two steps, then jerked his paw back when a drop of rain hit the fur.

"It's just rain," Victoria said, "I promise you'll live."

Charlie scratched at the studded rhinestone collar, and stayed put.

"See?" Victoria extended her palm past the porch roof, caught a few drops, then shook them off. "I didn't melt."

Victoria moved another step forward, down the stairs and onto the walkway. Rain sprinkled on her hair, dampening her shirt, her bare arms. "Come on, Charlie. You can do it."

Charlie laid his head on his paws.

"Oh, come here, boy." She bent to her knees, put out her arms. "I'll protect you."

Still, he didn't move.

She laughed. "Okay, I don't blame you. Wait here a second." She ran up the porch stairs, ducked inside and came back out with one of the umbrellas stored in the porcelain container by the door. With a flick of a button, the umbrella was extended into a black protective circle. "*Now* will you go out?"

Charlie looked up, noted the dry temporary ceiling, then marched forward, with Victoria keeping pace beside him. He did his business, then started back in the direction of the house. Just before they reached the porch, Charlie stepped back, as if he wanted to brave the rain one more time.

Several drops hit him square on the head. He shook them off, testing the feeling. Another drop, then another, spattered on his skinny back. He looked up at Victoria, then darted back under the shelter of the umbrella.

"That's okay, Charlie," Victoria said, laughing. "I'm taking baby steps, too."

She'd been successful with the dog. What were the chances the same techniques would work on his owner?

* * *

Noah had no idea how he got talked into taking Victoria into Boston. One minute he was eating French toast, slathering on the Vermont maple syrup and the next, he was suggesting a trip down the Freedom trail. It had come out of his mouth like it was all his idea, but he had a feeling that somehow, Victoria had been the one convincing him.

Last night, he'd left the room, adamantly opposed to the idea. But now, it didn't seem so bad. A way to pass the time until his truck was repaired.

Uh-huh.

Well, it was also the least he could do to repay her for the help, the room and the meals. He'd give her this trip, help her open the doors to her own dreams.

And then leave.

He figured he'd be back by noon—enough time to grab his truck and make his way up to Maine before the end of the day.

A trip to Boston wouldn't hurt his plans at all. And, he reasoned, it was a tourist spot he'd been meaning to visit anyway. Kill two avoidance techniques with one stone.

Yeah, right, his hormones whispered. If that was the case, then why was he standing by the front door, waiting for Victoria as eagerly as a sixteen-year-old about to go out on his first car date?

He'd shaved twice, changed his shirt three times, and spent more time brushing his teeth than he did when he was going to the dentist.

"Are you ready?" she said.

He turned and saw her descending the oak staircase, dressed in a dark blue skirt, flats and a soft pink sweater set that scooped slightly at her neck, revealing a plain gold chain with a simple heart pendant sliding along the links. On any other woman, the ensemble might have been called plain, ordinary.

But there was something about the light in Victoria's eyes, the smile that spread across her face, that made her transcend from ordinary to…

Well, the kind of woman he hadn't seen in a long, long time.

For an instant, she had him craving domesticity. Craving this sight, day after day.

If he knew what was good for him, he'd call the garage, pay Larry extra for a rush job, then hightail it to Maine.

Charlie, however, had other ideas. He crossed the wood floor, nails click-clacking, and went up to Victoria, tail wagging, nose eagerly sniffing the air, as if the dog who had whined and moaned nearly every mile between Rhode Island and Massachusetts was anticipating the ride in the car.

Like he was actually happy to go on a trip.

"You've charmed him," Noah said.

Victoria looked down at the dog and grinned. "Charlie and I have worked out an agreement."

"An agreement?"

"Yep. I'll hold an umbrella over him on the rainy days, and he'll be nice."

"That dog is about as nice as a wild boar. Remember my sock? Someone's going to lay out to get a tan this year and come up with a crew sock covered in dog slobber."

"Oh, you just have to know how to handle him. He's a sweetheart, really." She bent down, scratched behind

Charlie's ears. He rolled onto his back, completely submitting to her touch.

He laughed. "And here I'd planned to use him to scare off the bears in Maine."

She grinned. "Too late. I think I've ruined him for you."

And she had. When it came time to leave, Noah had a feeling Charlie would stage a revolt.

"Sorry, boy," Victoria said. "But today, you have to stay here. Boston's no place for a little guy like you." The dog gave her a downcast look, but erased it as soon as she tossed him a handful of Milk-Bones.

Noah gave the dog a glare, but Charlie just flounced his tail and munched the treats into crumbs.

Victoria's ancient Chevy LeMans took a little coaxing to turn over. Once they were on the road, though, the car ran fine. As promised, Noah drove, following the street he'd been on the day before back through Quincy and then up to I-93. As they eased onto the highway, he noticed Victoria, her grasp on the dash like a steel trap, her hands white and tense.

"You okay?"

"Yep." She drew in a breath, relaxed her shoulders, then peeled her grip off the vinyl surface. "See?"

He had a feeling she was anything but fine. Still, he admired her moxie, her determination to plow forward, regardless of what worries were churning in her gut. Every time he looked over at her, she seemed to be holding it together a little bit better.

She was a hell of a woman. The kind of woman he had once imagined himself settling down with, forming the very things he'd never really had. A home. A family.

He shook off the thoughts. This woman, this house,

was a temporary stop, a glitch in his plan to become a hermit. Getting involved with Victoria didn't fit with a life of solitude. It was a little tough to be a hermit with a roommate.

At South Station, they dipped down into the tunnel, Victoria clearly still holding her nerves on a tight leash as they drove through the brightly lit crowning achievement of the Big Dig, then exited at Government Center. "From here," he said, glancing down at the map she'd had in the glove compartment, "we can take the scenic route over to Beacon Hill, or hit the Gardens, or—"

"Look! The Aquarium!" Victoria exclaimed, pointing at a blue sign on the road. "Let's go there."

"Your wish is my command, milady," he said, the words a flirt he didn't intend. But when she flashed a smile back at him, he forgot why that was such a bad idea. Heck, he forgot his own name.

Driving the streets of Boston wasn't anywhere near as dangerous as the tightening thread running between himself and Victoria Blackstone.

CHAPTER SEVEN

THE blowfish peered at Noah, one of his wide round eyes watching the odd human on the other side of the glass. The puffer spun to one side, flipping a fin—in greeting or in farewell, Noah had no idea, since he didn't speak Aquatic Animal—then swam off.

Noah and Victoria were standing by the large central tank in the New England Aquarium, much more in awe of the two hundred thousand–gallon structure than the schoolchildren beside them. Dozens of kids, all dressed in the same red school-branded T-shirt and sporting laminated name tags, darted up and down the carpeted path, having more fun avoiding their adult chaperones than peering into the glass.

Victoria stood there, mesmerized by the four-story high tank and the multihued coral reef anchoring the center. It was their third visit to the saltwater shelter, but every time seemed to reveal more than the time before. After this, Noah knew Victoria would want to go through all the gallery exhibits again, stop to wave at the sea lions, maybe gasp at the stunningly huge sharks again. Every trip they made through the museum, Victoria saw something new.

Her enthusiasm had bred a similar feeling in him. He found himself peering into the watery depths, wondering what might swim by next.

It was fun, something he hadn't had in a long time.

"Fish are a lot like people, don't you think?" Victoria touched the glass gently, leaning in closer. At the bottom of the tank, a lime-green moray eel hid himself inside the coral's crevices. "Every one of them is unique, but they need each other to survive."

He could quibble with the whole concept of needing others for survival, but he didn't. The last thing Noah wanted to do was wipe that smile of happiness off Victoria's face. She'd started out their day seeming a bit stressed, almost…confined by the crowds, but as the day wore on, everything about her had relaxed, making him feel the same. Maybe her trip into the city hadn't been as bad as she'd expected. "So where to next? Back to the penguins?"

She laughed. "I think we'll turn into merpeople if we stay here any longer. Let's go outside and grab some lunch."

"Good idea." Together, they headed out of the aquarium and onto the bustling red stone plaza. Above them, the noon sun bathed the lunch breakers in golden warmth.

Noah had planned to leave by now, to be heading for the solitude of Mike's cabin by early afternoon. He glanced over at Victoria, her face, like so many others, upturned to greet the afternoon rays.

When he was with Victoria, Maine seemed as far away as Jupiter. So did all the worries and disappointments that had hitched a ride in his truck. What would a few more hours hurt?

His gaze swept over the long curve of her neck, the hourglass curves below that, and then back up to the sweet pink lips that never seemed to be far from his mind.

The ocean breeze wrapped around them, warm and thick with salt. He inhaled, drawing the air into his lungs, making it a part of him.

"It's incredible, isn't it?" Victoria asked.

"What is?"

"The way the ocean makes you feel. Almost…" she paused, searching for the right word, "restored."

He drew in another breath, and for one moment, it seemed as if everything was right with his world. "It does."

At some point, they had started to hold hands. He couldn't remember when, or what had triggered him to take her palm with his own. Either way, her touch in his felt natural, perfect. He stopped in the plaza, spinning her against him. She collided lightly with his chest, surprised. A quick gasp of breath escaped her. "What is it about you?" he asked.

"What is it…?" She looked confused. "What do you mean?"

"You make me forget all my best intentions."

"Oh." She smiled. "I'm sorry." But she didn't seem sorry at all.

He watched her lips move, opening and closing like a rose about to bloom. Captivated, he leaned in closer. Then, before he could think better of it, he kissed her.

From somewhere in the distance, a seal barked. A car horn beeped. People meandered by, murmuring comments about public displays of affection.

But Noah barely heard it. The instant his lips had met hers, desire and need exploded within his chest.

He reached his hands up, tangling in her short bouncy locks, dancing along the tiny vertebrae of her neck. Her arms stole around his chest, then her tongue darted inside to play with his.

Want surged in Noah's chest, his brain, his mouth, deepening their kiss, taking it from a public display of affection to something dancing close to a little more.

Finally, one of them, he didn't know, didn't care who, pulled back and inserted some sanity into the space between them.

"We should…we should probably go," Victoria said.

His gaze went to the Marriott Hotel, just yards away. Every hormone in his body was pinging on that building, like a submarine sonar. "We should." She started to pull out of his arms, but he held her tight. "Uh, we have to wait a minute."

Confusion knitted her brows together.

"I…well, I'm not in any condition to walk around in public yet."

Heat flooded her face, tinting her cheeks scarlet. "Oh. *Oh.* I'm so sorry."

He chuckled. "It's not your fault. Blame it on Mother Nature."

He didn't mind the delay, either. It gave him time to study the face of this woman who was still, essentially, a stranger but who at the same time seemed as familiar as his own hand. In the depths of her eyes, he saw a kind of innocence that said she'd probably never dipped a toe into the darker waters of life. Noah had been treading water there far too long.

Stay, his mind whispered. *Stay and forget.*

The thought was tempting, as tempting as kissing her

again. Why not stay? Rent that room, start a new life, find a new job?

"We should get going," Victoria said again, drawing back a bit. "So we can get to the garage."

"The truck's not going anywhere." He looked around, spied a hot dog vendor a few feet away, the steam rising from the vents in the stainless steel cart. "Let's have lunch, sit on the pier for a while and just…" He threw up a hand, searching for the right word.

"Just be?"

He nodded, liking the sound of that. When had he ever just been? When had he ever sat anywhere, with no intentions besides soaking up the sun and his surroundings? "Yeah."

She grinned, slipped her hand back into his, and started wending her way through the crowds and over to the hot dog vendor. As they approached the cart, Noah opened his mouth to ask Victoria how she took her dogs, when something caught his eye.

A Brown University sweatshirt. Red, hooded, worn. Familiar.

It couldn't be. He turned back to the vendor, but his attention strayed a second time to the sweatshirt.

Maybe…it could.

"Justin?" Noah called out to the figure disappearing into the crowd. The hooded head shot a quick glance back, too fast for Noah to discern a face, an eye color, then ducked away.

Noah's breath froze in his chest. Time stood still, the plaza closing in around him, like a telescope focusing on a single star. That flash of red, now getting further and further away.

fusal was loud, sharp.

kstone was a grown woman. If she wanted
n on her own, she could very well do so.
re was something about her demeanor,
eyes, that kept him rooted to the stones
et. He thought of what she had told
childhood. This might be too much, too
one who had been as secluded as she.
n't feel right about leaving you here, es-
what you told me last night."

p relying on you. You're going to leave
aren't you?"

hit him like a slap. But they were the truth
ut it would only make it worse on both of
es."

ve to learn to do this on my own. So I'm
to leave." The smile on her face, though,
t, too chipper.

of training told him that she was right, that
teps on her own was the best way to help her
fe. But still… "You don't have to tackle the
one day. You can come back another time."
's today or never. This is important to me."
oah, before you get wrapped up even more.
replayed their kiss, the tender feel of her
the wonder on her face inside the aquarium,
of protectiveness rose within him, overrid-
other emotion. "You're not okay," he said,
hand, placing her keys back into them,
til she met his gaze squarely before speaking
d I'm not taking your car, no matter what you
m I leaving you here. Not alone."

Justin?

Propelled by instinct, he let go of Victoria's hand and
took off, his eyes riveted on the spot of crimson among
the dozens of people. The color, the logo of the school
Justin had dreamed of attending—before he'd hooked up
with the wrong crowd and traded ambition for trouble.

Noah ran, charging through the multitude of people,
gaining ground, getting closer with every step. He
reached, fingers extending, brushing against soft cotton,
almost…almost grasping the soft cloth. "Justin!"

But then the figure before him broke into a run,
darting across the busy street. Before Noah could see
which way he went, the red sweatshirt had been swallowed up by the lunchtime throng.

Gone. Out of his grasp.

Again.

"Noah?"

He turned and found Victoria beside him, concern
etched on her features. Too late, he realized he'd aban-
doned her. "I'm sorry I took off like that. I shouldn't have
left you," he said. "I thought that was someone I knew."

"I'm okay," she said, and again, he saw the same well
of determination fill her features. But beneath it all, a
fine sheen of fear still showed. He kicked himself again
for leaving her. "What a coincidence that would be if it
was someone you knew, all the way in Boston."

Too much of one, Noah decided. Yet, he could have
sworn that he'd seen Justin, in everything from the
loping step to the hunched shoulders.

His heart constricted with worry, wrapping a tight
band around his chest. If it had been Justin, what was
he doing here? And if it hadn't been…

Where the hell was Justin right now?

Noah closed his eyes, willing his mind not to show the possibilities. But they reflected before him all the same: Justin, curled up on a piece of cardboard beneath an overpass, shivering in the evening cold. Running down a dark street. Laying in a hospital somewhere, beaten, bloody.

Alone.

"Are you all right?" Victoria's light touch on his shoulder, her voice soft in his ear. Drawing him away from the dark and back into the light of day.

He cleared his throat. It hadn't been Justin. It couldn't have been. The last report he'd had, two days ago, the fourteen-year-old boy had been in Providence, hanging with the gang that had turned him from a grumpy adolescent into a lost, defiant teen. There was no way Justin would have left his "boys" to head to Boston. "Yeah. Let's get that hot dog now."

She shot him a quizzical glance, but let it go. They paid for two hot dogs, slathered on the condiments, but the happy mood between them had evaporated like rain on a summer sidewalk.

He crossed the plaza, tossed their trash into a can, then dusted his hands together. "Ready to go?"

Victoria's smile seemed forced, strained. "Where to next?"

Away from here, was Noah's only thought. He'd been playing at a game he didn't deserve to play, one that involved someone else…and could lead to him hurting Victoria. The best thing to do was leave.

He'd thought he could pretend he was a regular man for a day, but what had just happened reminded him that

he couldn't. As
that included a
much baggage a

"Back to the h
then head over to
ready by now. An
back for the truck

Victoria avoide
into her pocket, p
them over to Noah
need to get to a rer
I'll have Mrs. With

"What about you
She wrapped her
draw in, into herself–
I'm going to tackle th

Yet as she said the
adding a shake to the
in her gaze. The tensi
stiffened her limbs. He

"I don't want to leav
get home."

"I need to do this, N
bottom lip, and for a sec
or change her mind. He t
but before he could oper
that determined side again
or the T or something." A
but like her earlier smile, it
worse comes to worst, I'll

"That's crazy. Let me
you—"

"No!" Her re
Victoria Blac
to wander Bosto

And yet, the
the look in her
beneath his fe
him about her
soon, for som
"Victoria, I do
pecially after

"I can't ke
soon anyway,

The words
and lying abo
them later. "

"Then I h
ordering you
was too brig

His years
taking these
change her l
whole city in

"Nope, it
Leave, N

His min
hand in his,
and a rush
ing every
taking her
waiting un
again, "an
say. Nor a

There went his plan for staying uninvolved.

"You *have* to, Noah." She drew her palm out of his and for a second, watched a woman pushing a stroller, crossing the pier and chatting with her baby as if the child could understand every word. "Besides, if you want to get your truck before the garage closes, you better go now. It's Saturday and Larry likes to knock off early to go to the Sox game. He lives in perpetual hope of another World Series win."

Noah looked around the busy area, then back at Victoria. "You still want to stay here alone?"

She nodded, too fast. "Yep."

He should take her at her word. After all, if there was anything he'd learned in the last year, it was that he really stunk at helping people, protecting them. Undoubtedly Victoria was much better at taking care of herself than he would be. But still…he worried.

"Here," he said, pressing his cell phone into her hand. "I'll take a cab. Call me if anything happens, if you don't feel like driving back, if you need toothpicks—" at that, she gave him a faint grin "—and I'll come back."

"Noah, I—"

"I won't take no for an answer," he said, echoing her words from earlier. Then, even though he knew she was a grown adult, some gene within him compelled him to give her advice. "Now, be careful, watch for—"

"Strangers, eat my vegetables and look both ways before crossing the street. I know. I appreciate you caring—"

He didn't care, he told himself. He was just being a good tenant.

"But I really want to do this on my own. So go." She gave him a gentle push in the direction of the street, where cabs whizzed by.

Noah did as she asked, but as he walked away, he had the distinct feeling it was a huge mistake.

After Noah was out of sight, Victoria drew in a deep breath to steady herself. Then another one. A third.

The crowds that had seemed so friendly before suddenly took on a menacing cast beneath the clouds that had moved in, blocking the sun. The ocean breeze, warm and balmy earlier, turned cold and bitter as it whistled against the buildings, slinking through her clothes. The noises of the street, which she had once considered background music when she was with Noah, became blaring horns and screeching tires.

Her heart raced, her pulse thundering so loud in her head, she thought surely every person in a hundred-foot radius could hear it.

"I can do this," she whispered to herself. "I *have* to do this."

It was utterly ridiculous that a thirty-year-old woman should be a nervous wreck leaving the house by herself. Since she'd been okay when she was with Noah, she'd thought she'd gotten over that anxiety, as if she'd just woken up one day and the past years had been wiped away.

Clearly they hadn't been. She drew in several short, fast gulps of air, then sank onto the bench, grasping the hard stone edge.

Enough. Today she would get around this city, do it by herself. Last week, she'd mailed out dozens of job applications. If one of those companies hired her, she'd have to do this every day.

Victoria forced her breathing to slow, willing her pulse to stop its frenzied rush. Yet, still, every person around her, every building, every honking horn, only added to her anxiety and the tightening coil of her nerves.

She drew in a breath of determination, got to her feet and strode forward before she could think about it. Despite being outdoors, the suffocating lunchtime crowds were almost claustrophobic. But she pressed forward, resolute.

Across the way, she spied the famous Haymarket Square, brimming with street vendors selling fruits, vegetables, flowers and almost everything under the sun. It was busy there, too, women hurrying by, clad in business suits and Nikes, men hefting briefcases stuffed to the gills, virtually everyone carrying on conversations via earbuds and cell phones. It looked fun and terrifying all at the same time.

A low breath escaped her lips. The marketplace seemed a million miles away, far across a congested labyrinth. Her feet froze in place, refusing to move.

She glanced down at the cell phone clutched in her hand. Her link to Noah. To rescue.

A rescue she refused to need.

Victoria inhaled, then let her breath out with a whispered prayer. She looked both ways at the insanely busy traffic, crossed first Atlantic Avenue, then Surface Road. She moved quickly, before she could think about what she was doing, skirting through the side streets, following her nose and the signs. Before the last turn, she paused, trying to regain her bearings. When she did, the scents, noise and congestion assaulted her, slamming against already frayed nerves.

She stumbled back, colliding with someone who let out a curse at her clumsiness, then pushed forward, crossing a side street and climbing onto the sidewalk and into the lunchtime fray.

The cell phone pressed against her palm, hard and cold. No. She'd be damned if she'd call Noah. She was a grown woman, after all, and even if the thought of being here sent worries piling on top of her like football players trying to squash a pigskin, she decided she would, indeed, do this.

And when she'd conquered the fear, she was going to go to the best shoe store in town and splurge. Surely, after a day like this, a woman deserved a new pair of slingbacks.

And hopefully not a heart transplant, too.

CHAPTER EIGHT

NOAH had every intention of going to Larry's garage, picking up his truck, loading it up and getting the heck out of Dodge. He'd called Dan, asking if there'd been any reports of Justin leaving town, but Dan said no, far as he knew, the boy was still hanging with the gang.

The boy he'd seen hadn't been Justin, he told himself. He'd heard somewhere that everyone had a twin in the world. That's all it was, Justin's doppelganger.

He could stop worrying about that. But he couldn't stop worrying about Victoria. She might have said she was going to be just fine, but something in his gut told him she might have overestimated herself.

The further the cab took him from the city, the more convinced Noah became that he was imagining things. Imagining his nephew. Imagining he'd read the very opposite of independence in Victoria's eyes.

The cab pulled up in front of Victoria's house. He asked the driver to wait, went inside to pick up Charlie, then got back into the car and gave the driver the address for Larry's garage.

Noah didn't realize until he was five miles down the

road that he'd left his duffel behind. A patent Freudian slip—or whatever psychologist it was who specialized in men who said one thing and did another.

Charlie had climbed into the back window of the red top and was now whimpering and scratching at the glass, as if he wanted to go back to Victoria. Who was Noah kidding? If he could have crawled into that back window and whined until he was back with Victoria, he would have, too.

He wanted her. In a way that went beyond lust and bordered on the very kind of thing Noah had done a damned good job of avoiding all his life.

Commitment.

"Oh, hell," Noah said, then ordered the driver to turn the car around. Back toward the city. Back to Victoria.

He should never have left her, should have ignored her insistence that she'd be okay. When they hit Atlantic Avenue, Noah hopped out, tossed the driver far too much money and grabbed Charlie. He wrangled the dog, who was as slippery and evasive as an eel, into his leash, then started back toward where he'd last seen Victoria.

She wasn't at the aquarium. Along the boardwalk. Down Atlantic Avenue. Where had she gone? Why hadn't she called him? What if—

The possibilities, many of which he knew far too well after his years in the juvenile justice system, were too awful to consider. He shut them out and moved faster, his gaze scanning the crowd for a petite woman with dark hair. Then he caught the scent of fresh foods and knew exactly where Victoria would have gone.

Haymarket Square.

Charlie strained forward on the leash, even as Noah

increased his pace. They navigated the side streets, not stopping for any of the women gushing about Charlie's looks. The dog just tipped his nose higher in the air.

Noah weaved through the crowds, the buildings, looking for Victoria. As he stepped into the market, the crush of people quadrupled. Charlie squirmed in Noah's arms, but he held the dog tight, afraid he'd get trampled. The crowd bordered on a melee, with vendors screaming their prices, customers jostling for space. The voices were loud, the prices ridiculously low, the people more mosh pit than customers.

It was insanity—only with apples and tomatoes.

Where was Victoria? Had his instincts been wrong? Or worse, was she trying to call him right now, and he wasn't there to answer the phone? He scanned the crowd, Charlie still securely—and reluctantly—tucked against his chest, ignoring the shopkeeper who stepped in front of him, shouting something about having the best zucchini prices in town—

And saw her.

Huddled in an alcove, her arms tight around her chest. A bag brimming with vegetables and bunches of herbs stood at her feet.

"Victoria!" Noah strode over to her, unable to keep an overjoyed Charlie from leaping out of his arms and onto the ground, then dashing up to greet Victoria. Relief flooded him when they finally reached her. "Are you okay?"

"Yes." She sucked in a breath, then dipped her head in a move so vulnerable, he wanted to wrap her in his jacket and take her away from this city, this world.

"No, you're not okay," he said softly. "Talk to me."

"It's nothing. I'm just a little…overwhelmed by the crowds, that's all." But her voice had trembled when she spoke and her grip on his cell phone was white knuckled. Despite the bravado Victoria was trying to muster, she looked like her nerves had been scattered like buckshot.

"Come here," he said, reaching out and drawing her to him. She stayed there, against his chest. After a long moment, he felt her relax in his arms.

A second later, she drew back, sending starch back into her spine. "What are you doing here anyway? I didn't call you."

"I…" What was he supposed to say? He'd had a feeling?

Or the truth, that for the first time in months, his intuition had actually worked. For years, his gut had been his best tool in his job, telling him where a scared kid might hide out, where a runaway might head, when to pull a kid from a questionable family life. In the past year, though, his intuition had failed him, time and time again, like a TV that kept receiving the wrong channel no matter how much foil you wrapped around the antenna.

Telling her he'd had a gut feeling would undoubtedly make Victoria feel like a kid who'd wandered too far from the backyard. Not to mention, it would tell her he cared. That he worried about her. He was leaving, soon as he was sure she was home safe. Admitting those feelings would add another strut to that bridge he was trying so damned hard not to build. "Uh…Charlie missed you."

He was really getting desperate if he was blaming it on the dog.

She smiled down at the Chihuahua, who reveled in every ounce of her attention. His tail went into such hyperdrive, NASA could have used him to power the space shuttle. "Smart boy." Then she tipped her face to look at Noah. The color of her eyes deepened, drawing him in, stirring want and need in his gut. "Smart owner."

Noah reached up, caught a tendril of her dark hair and let it slip through his fingers. "Are you better now?"

"Yeah." The smile that crossed her lips socked him hard, sending tremors through an already earthquake-prone libido. "Thank you."

Two words, the kind that sales people tossed at you after you bought a screwdriver or a doughnut, and yet, coming from her, they took on deeper proportions.

"Good," he murmured, then before he could think about it, he drew her out of the alcove and back into his arms, pressing a kiss to lips that tasted of honey. Her body molded against his, like two jigsaw puzzle pieces finding the right corner.

Someone jostled them from behind and Noah moved back, releasing Victoria. Her smile laced through them again, then—

The hairs on the back of Noah's neck stood up, his mental TV tuning again to Intuition Station. He turned, his gaze sweeping the crowds, looking, he thought, for danger, for a threat, something he had seen far too often when he'd tracked down some kid in the bowels of Providence. Then, out of the corner of his eye, he saw the red sweatshirt again, the hood drawn over the head, the loping, easy step.

Justin.

He'd taken several steps in the direction of the boy

when he looked back at Victoria. In her eyes, he saw abandonment. Fear. Far more than a simple case of nerves.

Two cars were both vying for the same parking space in front of her. The owners had gotten out of their autos and were angrily debating ownership of the piece of tar. Spectators had gathered, enclosing the space in front of Victoria.

She had retreated to the alcove, her back nearly glued to the wall, Charlie clutched to her chest. The color had drained from her face, leaving her a pale imitation of the woman he had met two days ago.

What the hell had he been thinking, chasing a ghost? Victoria needed him, more than she wanted to admit. He pivoted back, letting the sweatshirt—and the boy wearing it—disappear among the winding streets of Boston.

"Come here," he said, reaching out to her. "Take my hand. We'll go back to the car together. I promise, I won't leave you again."

She hesitated, then placed her palm in his. Heat infused his skin, racing up his arm, winding something invisible, yet oddly tangible between them.

Noah knew, as he pulled Victoria toward him, that leaving this city, this woman, wasn't going to be as simple as releasing a slipknot. No, this tie was becoming more and more tangled by the minute.

"Thank you," she said again after they'd made their way to a quieter section of the street. "I got a little swamped by the crowds."

A little swamped? He didn't say it, but to his eyes, she looked like she'd been caught in a storm. He held tight to her hand, keeping her close as they made their way back to where her car was parked.

Once more, Noah scanned the people around them, but the red sweatshirt was nowhere to be seen. Either Justin had moved on, or the whole thing had been a figment of Noah's imagination.

The woman beside him, however, was a reality that Noah hadn't counted on. His best laid plans had just been disrupted—by his own heart.

This was the last thing Victoria had expected Noah to do.

When they got back to the house, she'd thought he'd pack that duffel, heft it over his shoulder and head on out the door. But instead of calling a taxi or Larry, he'd picked up the phone and ordered—

A pepperoni pizza.

"You sit," he said, leading her to the sofa. Charlie hopped up on the other end, settling himself so close to Victoria, he could have been glued there. "Stay," he ordered with a grin, placing the remote in her hand.

"But—"

"But nothing. You had a hell of a day and I think you deserve to put your feet up, and let someone else do the dishes."

She grinned. "Are you going to call in the shoe-maker's elves?"

"Hey, I've got a few kitchen skills. Meaning, I can pick up the phone."

"And order pizza."

He returned the grin. "Of course."

Victoria did as Noah said, staying on the sofa, flicking channels with the remote. But nothing on the TV interested her nearly as much as the man who was in her kitchen, washing the breakfast dishes. It felt really weird to be the one waited on, while he brought her a glass of ice water, paid the pizza guy and then dished them each up hearty slices of pepperoni.

But it was definitely a feeling she could get used to. She may have been unnerved by the city experience, but she wasn't completely crazy.

"What got you feeling all domesticated?" she asked when he sat down beside her, each of them holding paper plates loaded with the meaty pie. She said the words like a joke, but really, she wanted to know what had made him step in and take care of her…like a husband would.

"You had a hard day, Victoria, and I wanted to make it end easy."

She waved her hand in dismissal. "All I did was get a little scared by the crowds. Now, it feels silly."

He laid his plate on the coffee table, then took her hands in his. "It isn't silly. You wouldn't expect someone who had never gotten behind the wheel of a car to all of a sudden drive like a pro."

"True."

"Then you shouldn't expect so much out of yourself. One step at a time," he said, unknowingly echoing her words to herself earlier. Only hers had also ended with the thought of a wedding aisle.

Irony, in its purest form. Because the idea that had seemed so far-fetched to her earlier was looking more and more attractive the longer she was around Noah.

"What about you?" she asked, diverting the subject— and her thoughts—away from dangerous territory. "Why are you chasing a teenager around the streets of Boston?"

Noah heaved a sigh. "Because he's my responsibility."

She weighed the question in her mind before asking, because she wasn't so sure she wanted to know the answer, to know this man had a wife, a family. "Is Justin your son?"

"No, my nephew. My brother is in Iraq, on his second tour of duty. Before he got called up, he named me as Justin's legal guardian."

She took a bite of the pizza, digesting the information with the food. "I don't understand. If that's the case, then why did you leave him behind in Providence?"

"He left me." Noah settled back against the sofa, draping one arm over the back, but looking far from comfortable. It struck her how little she knew about this stranger temporarily living in the back bedroom of her house. If she were smart, she'd stay out of his problems. Dealing with her own was enough for now. And yet, there was something about Noah that compelled her to ask.

To care.

"What happened?"

"It's the typical story. Justin started running with the wrong crowd when he was twelve. Ended up joining a gang at thirteen, about the same time Robert went to Iraq for the first time. I tried everything I could to get Justin out of there, even enrolling him in a gang counseling program, but…" His voice trailed off and this time, it was her turn to comfort him, to slide closer and put her arm across his, waiting. "None of it worked. He just kept going back to the gang, running off for days at a time, dabbling in drugs, petty crime. No matter what I did, I couldn't get through to him."

"Is that where he is now?"

Noah nodded. "He took off again a few days ago, after I'd chased him into the woods, trying like hell to get him to stop, to listen to reason."

"Then why did you leave Providence? Why not track him down again?"

"Because this time, when he took off, he made it clear he wanted nothing to do with me. I figured we both needed some space."

Her gaze swept over him, adding up the pieces of Noah that she had gathered so far in the last few days. "And you needed some time to figure out where you went wrong."

"Yeah, I guess I did," he said. "Dan, my boss, is watching over him, but Justin is so far sucked into that gang, I don't know if anyone can get him out again. The kid seems determined to ruin his life."

"I know that feeling," she said softly. "In the weeks that led up to my parents' deaths, the doctors told me the whole thing was inevitable. There wasn't any miracle cure that would come along and stop this from happening. And still, at the very end, in those last breaths—" Her voice cut off, and Noah gripped her hand, tight, giving her support, telling her he knew, without her finishing the story. Yet, she needed to, if only to get the words out, to finally tell someone all of it. "Even when I knew better, I kept hoping that it would end differently. That they wouldn't leave me."

Her voice broke on those last words and Noah reached out, drawing her into his arms as he had earlier that afternoon, pressing her face to the softness of his T-shirt, his solid body offering comfort, a shoulder. She didn't cry, but she absorbed every ounce of this man, a man who seemed to read her mind and fill in the gaps of her emotional recipes.

"Hope isn't a bad thing to have," he said quietly. "That's why I left. Because my hope had run out."

"But today," she said, raising her head, connecting with his gaze, "today, you thought you saw Justin?"

He nodded. "Yeah, but I called Dan and he said he heard the kid is still in Providence, far as he knows. Besides, what are the chances, that of all the places, Justin would come here?"

"Did he know you were going to Maine?"

Noah closed his eyes and drew in a breath. "Yeah. It was supposed to be a trip for the two of us. Male bonding and all that, except with fishing poles and s'mores. But in the end, he refused to go." He let out a heavy breath. "That's why I've decided to go back to Providence, soon as my truck is ready. I can't go to Maine while he's still out there. What was I thinking?"

She smiled softly. "You were thinking that all you wanted to do was get away from this for a while. As if, by doing so, it would all magically fix itself."

"How do you know me so well?" He tipped her chin up, bringing their lips inches apart. She could feel the steady warmth of his breath, feel the beat of his heart. "It's like you popped a hole in my brain and looked inside."

"I think it's because we've both lost people we care about. Just before my parents died, I took off, too," she said.

"You left? The house?"

She nodded. "Yeah and it went about as well as today did. I thought if I could just get into the city, get away from here, it would change things. So I called a cab, headed into Boston and ended up a crying wreck in Government Center. I was quite the tourist attraction."

"Oh, Victoria," he said, his green eyes filled with kindness, compassion. He drifted his thumb over her lips, then placed a sweet, soft kiss on her mouth. "You're a brave woman."

"Me? I'm the biggest scaredy-cat I know." She gave him a teasing grin, hoping to lift the mood, the heated tension twisting between them. "You know, I'm supposed to be through worrying about people, Noah, but then here you are, needing a worrier more than anyone I've ever met."

He shook his head. "I don't need anyone worrying about me. I can take care of myself."

"Uh-huh. You're doing such a fine job of it right now." She pressed a palm against his arm. Beneath her fingers, she could feel the worry tight in his muscles. "And, it's about time you did something about it. Dr. Victoria prescribes plenty of good times."

"I—"

"Don't argue. I can be very stubborn when I want to be."

"Victoria, I—" He cut himself off. "I'm not going to win this, am I?"

"Nope." She grinned.

"You know, I had a perfectly good evening of pity planned."

So had she. But doing so wouldn't move her one inch closer to her goal.

"Save it for a rainy day." She glanced out the window at the storm still blowing through, then laughed. "Well, another rainy day. Because you and I have plans."

CHAPTER NINE

THE kitchen had no visitors Saturday night. Noah lay in his bed, waiting to hear Victoria walk by on her way downstairs—and also hoping she didn't.

As each day had passed and he remained here, he became more and more entangled, not just in her life, but in his heart. He'd started to care about her. To worry. To spend time thinking about ways he could surprise her.

That night, on the sofa, he'd opened up to her, let her into his heart, and she had done the same. He'd begun to think they could make this work, that maybe…

But no, he wasn't the kind of man who should be in a relationship. Hell, he could barely control the few he had right now. Adding a woman like Victoria, a woman who deserved the whole enchilada, wasn't fair to her.

If they ended up in that kitchen again, he was sure—no, he knew—they would go way beyond kissing. Because most of all, he had begun to need her, not just in the way a man needs a woman, but in the ways one person needed another.

So he stayed in his bed, and so, he was sure, did she,

"What plans?"

"Change." She got to her feet, pulling him up with her. "Let's start here. Move the furniture around. Change the outlook."

"And you'll change the result?"

She grinned. "Or at least the view. It's better than sitting here and moping about things we have no control over."

He took an end of the couch and hefted it up. "Couches, those I can control."

And the beat of her heart, she thought as they moved the sofa to a new place in front of the double-hung windows. Because every time she looked at Noah McCarty, her heart rate doubled.

keeping them from a moonlight encounter that would only draw the threads around them tighter.

When the sun crested over the horizon, he pulled on some clothes and went downstairs. A second later, Victoria entered the kitchen, this time wearing jeans, a white T-shirt and a large, thick denim shirt that seemed to dwarf her petite frame. "Good morning," he said.

"Good morning." She glanced out the window. "Rain is still coming down."

"I was thinking I'd head into the city again this morning, retrace our steps."

"Want some company?"

Yes, his mind screamed. He wanted her with him today, tomorrow and the next day. He didn't want to wake up another morning without seeing her smile in his kitchen. "No, I'm fine. You probably have stuff around here to get accomplished."

A pained look filled her eyes but she turned away quickly and got to work making coffee. "Sounds like a good idea."

"Listen, I don't want you to think—"

"I don't, Noah, don't worry." Her words were sharp, tight.

"Victoria," he said, reaching to turn her back to face him, knowing he had to get the words out now. Before he couldn't find the guts to say them. "I don't want to give you the impression that I'm staying. That I can be anything more than a temporary boarder. I have to go back to Providence."

"I know. And I have to move forward, too." She put on a smile, but he got the feeling her heart wasn't in it. "So I'm fine with you doing your thing and I'll do mine."

He wished then that he *had* gone down into the kitchen in the middle of the night. That he *had* swept her into his arms and kissed her. Because right now, getting more involved with Victoria seemed like a much better option than trying to push her away.

Or at least that's what he told himself as he climbed into the LeMans and took off for a gloomy city.

Victoria drew in a deep breath, extended the umbrella, then took a step off the porch. Charlie took a hesitant step beside her, making sure he stayed under the security of the umbrella.

"It's just a trip to the corner market," she told the dog, glad for his company. Charlie hadn't wanted to go out in the rain, but Victoria urged him to go, if only for his own good, too. "I need some chocolate."

The dog yipped, as if he could understand cravings. He trotted along beside her, a perfect companion for her rainy three-block walk. Along the way, she was sloshed by a speeding car—which made Charlie nearly turn tail and run back home—and then almost got run over by a teenager taking a turn too fast.

But she made it. There and back, with a couple packages of cookies and a full gallon of milk. It was another step forward, which heartened her for the days ahead. As scary as yesterday had been, it had clearly been good for her.

As she hung up her raincoat, she caught a glimpse of Noah's sweatshirt, hanging in the closet. She ran a hand down the soft gray fabric. She told herself it was just as well he'd gone into the city alone. All she needed to do was wrap her heart around his even more.

Yeah, right. Then why did she feel this sharp, agonizing pain whenever she thought of that sweatshirt being gone?

She may have changed the living room, gone to the corner market and convinced a Chihuahua that he wouldn't die in the rain, but she had yet to find a way to prepare her heart for his eventual departure.

When Noah returned several hours later, Victoria had consumed half of the package of cookies, but it hadn't seemed to quench her craving. She stood against the kitchen counter, brewing a pot of coffee for additional dunking. "Did you find him?"

Noah shook his head and plopped into the seat across from her. "Not a sign." He reached into his pocket and pulled out a small brown paper bag. "But I did buy you a washer."

"How romantic," she said, teasing him. In the midst of all his worries, he'd thought about her sink. Either because he cared about her—or because the continual plopping had been torturing him.

"Hey, I'm nothing if not practical. Now where are those pink tools?"

"I can do it, if you want. I know how. I've fixed faucets before."

He rose and crossed to her, laying the paper bag on the counter behind her. He was close, so close she could almost hear his heart beat. Every fiber in her being wished that he would bend down, capture her lips again and make her forget all the very good reasons she'd had earlier for not getting involved with him. Jeez, it was no wonder she'd needed so much chocolate today. "And I can feel like I'm repaying you for your hospitality by fixing it for you."

She stepped away, trying to hide the hurt in her eyes. Repaying her for her hospitality? Is that all he saw it as?

As she left the room to retrieve the tools, Victoria told herself that putting distance between her and Noah was smart. He'd be gone soon as Monday came and Larry's garage was open again.

He was, as he'd said, a temporary boarder. And she had a permanent life change to live, one that didn't involve a man at her side.

Noah had perfected the art of not sleeping. Even though he spent Sunday fixing Victoria's faucet and then installing the glass in Mrs. Witherspoon's new greenhouse, he went to bed physically exhausted but had ended up lying awake most of Sunday night.

Listening again for Victoria's step. Thinking of how she'd looked in that nightgown. Picturing her smile, her eyes. Everything.

He'd done the right thing yesterday, by putting some distance between them. As morning dawned, he realized it was Monday, and the truck would undoubtedly be ready. Doing anything that might prolong his leaving, or might give hope to Victoria that this was more than a temporary stop, would be wrong.

And yet, when he went down to the kitchen and found her there, babying the recalcitrant coffeepot into one more brew, he knew, as well as he knew his own name, that the link that bound him had nothing to do with needing a place to sleep. And a lot to do with the attraction he felt for this woman.

An attraction that was building. Expanding. And lying squarely on the railroad tracks of his intentions.

She pivoted to face him. "Mrs. Witherspoon came by this morning and gave me two tickets for the Philharmonic Friday night. She told me to take a date, and I'm sure, knowing her matchmaking tendencies, that she meant you. Would you like to go?"

"I appreciate the offer," Noah said, and for a split second, considered saying yes, considered staying indefinitely, "but I'll be on my way well before then."

"I understand," she said, laying the two slim tickets on the counter, then busying herself with pouring each of them a cup. She stirred a bit of sugar into hers, still avoiding his gaze. "And it's probably better for me to try to make that trip alone. I'll take a cab, in case you're worried about my driving. In fact, I'm going to try cabbing it into the city today, too."

"Another tour of the Aquarium?"

"Nope." A smile spread across her face. "A job interview. It's nothing much, just some secretarial and receptionist work for a financial firm in Boston, but—"

"It's a start," Noah said. "Good for you." He put his mug down, then crossed to her, unable to resist those deep blue eyes, that bewitching smile. "Listen, it's Monday. Traffic is always doubly insane on Mondays. Why don't you let me take you?"

"You've done enough," she said. "And besides, I have to do this on my own. Ordinary people all over the world get jobs, commute back and forth and make life-changing decisions without a second thought or a chauffer. Relying on you will only delay the inevitable—"

He knew the end of the sentence before she even said it.

"You leaving," she said.

The two words hung in her kitchen, heavy and thick as the moist air that held another waiting storm. It wasn't raining, not yet, but Noah knew it would soon.

Oh, hell. He wanted to fix this, to return things to the way they had been earlier between them.

Across from him, Victoria flicked on a small fifties-style radio, tuning the dial until she hit an oldies station, probably trying to fill the uncomfortable silence.

An upbeat melody carried through the kitchen, sweeping through Noah's veins.

Ordinary people all over the world didn't just get jobs, they enjoyed their lives, in brief snippets. He could do that, too, for just a moment.

Before he could think about what he was doing, he stepped forward, scooped Victoria into his arms and began to dance. She let out a short gasp of surprise, but quickly fell into step with him.

They swung around the linoleum floor, Victoria's head thrown back, laughter pouring from her. Never had he met anyone like her, someone who found joy in every element of her life.

How he wanted to capture a little of that. He watched her every move, unwittingly following the words of the song. He swung her forward, into his chest, then spun her out. Then the song slowed and words of love filled the room.

Victoria spun back into Noah's arms, the words whispering their magic around the pair. At the same time, each of them stopped moving, their gazes locked together as firmly as their hands.

I love you.

Noah heard the words, both the ones in the song and the ones resonating in his own mind. They tickled at the edge of his lips. All he'd have to do was open his mouth and they'd be true.

Instead he cleared his throat. "You, ah, better get ready for that job interview." He gave her a grin he didn't feel. "Don't want to be late and make a bad impression."

But as he watched Victoria walk out the room, he got the distinct feeling he was the one making the bad impression.

CHAPTER TEN

VICTORIA tried like heck not to think about that impromptu dance in the kitchen as she changed into the business suit she'd bought three months ago through mail order. The suit skimmed nicely over her body, the straight skirt ending just at her kneecaps. Perfect.

The clothes were right, but the moment with Noah had gone as wrong as one possibly could. What had he been thinking when they'd stopped dancing and the words "I love you" boomed from the radio?

She'd been standing there, as if listening to the song would make the words come true. As if she wanted them to be true.

She shook her head and brushed the thoughts away. It was nerves, that's all. As soon as the phone call had come this morning from the Lincoln Corporation, she'd been on edge, wondering if she'd do this right—or end up cowering in an alcove with a Chihuahua.

Not exactly the best way to impress the department heads at Lincoln.

Victoria slid on the matching pumps she'd ordered. They didn't match the perfection of the suit and felt more like they'd been designed by the Marquis de Sade. Victoria ended up putting on a pair of black flats, which also served to take her confidence down a notch. She'd wanted everything to be perfect today, and already the shoes weren't. So much for the interview advice she'd found online about standing tall and commanding authority and confidence.

Okay, so she'd just stand on her tiptoes.

She went out to the kitchen, poured a glass of water and downed it, hoping to swallow her nervousness. What she got was a full, sloshing belly.

On the countertop, Noah's cell phone started to vibrate. She looked outside and saw him hammering planks onto a bench for Mrs. Witherspoon's newly revised and smaller patio. Mrs. Witherspoon watched, pausing every few minutes from her bulb planting. Victoria suspected she just liked seeing Noah flex his muscles. Heck, Mrs. Witherspoon wasn't the only one.

On the countertop, the vibrating stopped, then started again. She stepped closer, reading the caller ID through the little window on the front. "Dan."

Noah's boss. She knew that already from the first time he'd called. She calculated the distance to Noah. At most, the phone would ring five times before going into voice mail, or worse, the caller gave up. Even running, she doubted she could get the phone across two backyards and into Noah's hands before the rings subsided and the call was lost.

Before the third vibrating ring ended, Victoria flipped open the phone. "Hello?"

"Noah?"

"No, he's—"

"Can you give him a message?" Dan paused for a fraction of a second, just long enough for her to say yes. "I only have a second because I'm heading into court this morning. I got a lead on Justin. Apparently, he went to Boston. I don't know why, but he's there. I called the local cops and let them know, but it'd be better for the kid if Noah found him first."

"We've seen him," Victoria said, telling Dan about the encounter yesterday. She was now convinced that it had been Noah's nephew in the crowds.

"I'll be damned. Maybe he's looking for Noah."

"Trouble is, I don't think Noah would know what to say to him if he found him." She drew in a breath and decided confiding in his boss wouldn't be such a bad idea. The man, despite his abrasiveness, clearly cared about Noah and his nephew. "He doesn't think he's the right one to talk to him."

"The right one? Hell, he's the only one. Let me tell you something about Noah," and then Dan did, proceeding to share war stories from his years of working with Noah.

A few minutes later, they ended the call. Victoria closed the cell, then watched Noah out the window for a moment. She'd heard the same thing in Dan's voice that she'd seen in the slump of Noah's shoulders, heard in the pacing of her halls.

Worry and need.

When Noah saw Victoria heading out to Mrs. Witherspoon's backyard with his cell phone clutched in her hand, he knew.

The news he'd been dreading had finally come. He

steeled himself, his grip on the hammer so tight and stiff he couldn't tell where his hand ended and the wood began. Mrs. Witherspoon, who'd been chattering about the best methods of attracting bluebirds to a backyard—not information he needed considering he never intended to be a two-point-five kids and white picket fence guy—stopped midsentence.

"Dan called," Victoria said. Mrs. Witherspoon said something about needing to tend to the laundry and headed toward the house.

Noah's heart stopped beating. His breath lodged in his throat, getting tangled up with the words. All he could do was nod.

"Justin is in Boston."

It took at least ten seconds for her words to penetrate the fog in his mind. Justin. In Boston.

That *had* been who he'd seen yesterday. Now, he was sure of it. Nevertheless, Boston was a huge city, filled with millions of people. The chances of him finding Justin again were slimmer than finding a toothpick in a forest.

And just about as easy to spot.

Noah picked up the hammer again and laid a plank into place on the next bench. He pulled a couple of nails out of the pouch around his waist and began hammering. "Doesn't matter. Tell Dan to come up here. If I know my nephew, the last person he wants to see right now is me."

"Maybe you're the perfect person to help him."

"No, I'm not." The hammer hit the nail, metal on metal releasing a high-pitched thud.

"Why not?"

"Because the chance of finding him again are one in a trillion." Ping went the nail beneath the hammer. "Because Justin won't talk to me, even if I do find him." Another ping. "And because…" His voice trailed off, the sentence lost in his hammering.

"If you find him and he won't come this time, you'll probably lose him forever," she finished for him.

Noah nodded, silent.

"So you're just going to give up?"

"No, I'm going to find someone better suited to the job."

Victoria watched him finish the plank, his mood as unreadable as a storm cloud. "Same as you'll let someone better suited to the job be the one I should fall in love with, right?"

He popped his head up, pausing in his work. "Fall in love?" he repeated.

"You think you're not good enough to find Justin. Not good enough to hang around and do more than just kiss me over a ham and cheese sandwich." She took a step forward. "Maybe, Noah McCarty, you need to let everyone else make their own decisions about whether or not they want to love you."

Then she turned on her heel and left the yard. She had a job interview to get to. This indecipherable, stubborn man made her crazy. The best thing to do was go into the city early, buy a killer pair of shoes and forget him.

Noah put down his hammer, brushed the sawdust off his pants and realized that he was a complete and total jerk.

That, apparently, also came with the bachelor apartment.

Victoria was only trying to help and he'd snapped at

her, blaming her for his own shortcomings. One of which appeared to be his total inability to relate to a woman.

He watched her stride across the two lawns, back to her house, and realized that despite his best intentions, he had started to care about her—

And she had clearly started to do the same for him.

A calming peace stole over him. With Victoria behind him, as worried about Justin as he was, there was hope. The one thing Noah had thought he'd never feel again.

Noah broke into a run, tearing across the two lawns and up to Victoria, reaching her just before she went inside the house, Charlie right beside her. "Victoria, wait!"

Without pausing, Victoria pulled open the screen door. "What?"

"Don't leave," he said. "Not without me."

"Why?" she asked, spinning around to face him. "Because you think I need to be baby-sat? Because you think I'm not a big enough girl to handle going to a job interview on my own? Or worse, because Mrs. Witherspoon put you up to it?"

Charlie plopped his miniature butt on the porch and looked up at Noah, his head cocked to one side, waiting for an answer, too.

"No. On all counts."

"Then what, Noah? Because you won't talk to me. You won't tell me anything." With the last few words, her voice slipped into a softer range.

He knew he didn't deserve a woman like her, someone who threw out second chances like free baseballs at a minor league game.

"Wait," he said again, letting out a gust. "Because I need you."

"Noah, I—" she pointed toward the city, not even finishing the statement.

"I know. The job interview." It was Victoria's turn, her chance to move forward with her life. He may not know her well, but he knew this interview was a huge, important step. He wasn't going to interfere with that. "Let me just drive you into the city. That way, you get to your appointment," he said. "And I can start looking for my nephew again. And maybe after we're both done—" he paused a second "—we can try dancing again."

He meant much more than dancing, but didn't say it. Not now, not when everything around him was in such a fragile state.

Her blue eyes met his, reflecting the ocean. When it did, her gaze softened, causing his chest to tighten. "Interviews can be rescheduled," she said quietly. "Finding lost boys can't. I'll help you find him."

Hope took flight in his chest for the first time in a very, very long time. Victoria was the light for a world that he had seen as dark for far too long. "You don't have to do that."

"No, I don't have to. But I want to." She gestured toward the passenger side of the car. "Hop in," she said. "Because this time I'm driving."

He grinned, feeling positive for the first time all day. "In that case, I better buckle my seat belt."

CHAPTER ELEVEN

"WHY couldn't you be a bloodhound?" Noah asked Charlie while the three of them walked the same streets as they had on Saturday. Victoria had managed, with a lot of encouragement and direction from Noah, to make it—slowly—into the city and park again on Atlantic Avenue. He'd told her to think of the beeping horns behind her as music to drive to, which had made her laugh, and helped ease the tension in her shoulders.

The Monday afternoon commuter foot traffic was heavy and thick, which meant Charlie ended up getting a ride in Noah's arms more often then he had to put his dainty paws on the concrete.

The Chihuahua lifted his little nose in the air, apparently proud of his tiny pedigree, even if it lacked a good tracking nose.

"Where do you think Justin went?" Victoria asked.

He'd called and updated the cops on what he'd seen but they hadn't had any reports of finding anyone that matched Justin's description. They'd promised to keep an eye out for him but Noah knew as well as they did that if a teenager didn't want to be found…he wouldn't be. "Could be anywhere. A flop house, a shelter, an alley…"

"Or worse," she finished.

"Yeah. Or worse." He shuddered to think of where his nephew might be, of him feeling hungry, scared. "I'll start with the vendors in the area where we last saw him, and work outward from there."

"Sounds like a plan." She grinned.

"Victoria," he said, taking her hand, waiting until she looked at him, stopping on the sidewalk, much to the consternation of people trying to get by them. "This is my problem, not yours. I was wrong to ask you to help. If you leave now, you can still make that job interview."

She put out her hand. "Let me have your cell phone." When he gave it to her, she punched in a number, then waited for the other line to pick up. "This is Victoria Blackstone. I'm scheduled for a one-thirty interview with Mr. Lincoln. A family emergency has come up and I need to reschedule." She paused, waiting a moment. "Friday at two? That would be fine. Thank you." Then she hung up the phone and handed it back to him.

"Family emergency?"

"You're living in my house and your nephew is missing. I say that's close enough to a family emergency."

For a moment, the feeling that he and Victoria were a family soared through him. It sent a hundred pictures through his mind—pictures he'd have to deal with later. Maybe it was the sunny day. Maybe it was the streets they were walking, which had been traversed by his nephew just a couple days before.

Or maybe it was the woman standing next to him, so

clearly in his corner that he could stop feeling like he had to bear the entire load himself.

His ex-fiancée, Melissa, had never been like that. To her, his job was an inconvenience, a total waste of time and talent. Eventually his determination to help teens and hers to push him into the corporate world eroded their relationship. Since then, he hadn't met anyone who understood him and his work, until Victoria.

"You're amazing, you know that?" He took a step closer to her, brushing his fingertips against her cheek. The touch was tender, filled with words he couldn't say. The kind of words that would take this beyond a casual few-day encounter and into the realm of white picket fences.

"Amazing? Me?" She laughed, taking Charlie into her own arms when the little dog took the opportunity to jump off the Noah ship. "I'm about as ordinary as they come. A hundred percent homespun."

"And a rarity in the world I come from," he said.

She placed a quick, chaste kiss on his cheek. He wanted more, wanted to turn her face to his so he could capture those sweet pink lips once more. "And I think you've been out in the rain too long."

"I disagree with—" He cut the sentence off, his gaze caught again by a flash of red behind Victoria. A little dirtier red today than the day before, but the distinctive color all the same.

"What is it?" Victoria asked.

"There. That sweatshirt." He craned his neck, trying to see more than a hood and a baggy shirt. The figure turned to the left, moving to cross the street. When he did, Noah noticed the backpack dangling from one hand. Brown and tan. One broken strap. The exact same one Noah had ordered for Justin from Land's End, two Christmases ago.

And then, as the figure crossed the street and headed west, Noah saw his features.

"Justin!" He went to dash after the boy, but stopped when he thought of Victoria. He turned back for her.

"Go!" she said. "I'll follow."

He still hesitated.

"I'll be okay. Go."

Noah didn't hesitate another second. He broke into a run. "*Justin!*"

Justin looked back, over his shoulder, saw Noah coming, and for a fraction of a second, hesitated. Noah gained ground, closing the gap, but before he could reach him, Justin started, then sprinted away. Fifteen years and thirty pounds difference from the boy slowed Noah down, but Victoria, with her lithe, trim body, easily sailed up beside him, even with the dog still in her arms. "It's him," Noah said.

The clouds above burst open, releasing a drenching shower that caused Charlie to bark and people to scatter, using everything from that day's *Globe* to briefcases to cover their heads.

"I think he's heading for the T," Victoria said, one palm over her head, blocking the rain. Ahead of them, the distinctive green and orange signs marking Haymarket Square station seemed to glow like a beacon in the gray, dreary rain. And, just as Victoria had predicted, they saw Justin clamber down the stairs and into the station.

"Justin! Wait!" Noah shouted, then cursed when the red sweatshirt disappeared from view.

"We'll go down there, take separate directions. You

head for the Green line trains, I'll take Orange." She laid a hand on his arm and caught his gaze for an instant. "We'll find him, Noah."

With that, they plunged into the station, pursuing a lost boy who didn't want to be found.

Having exact change was a lot more handy than people realized; Victoria had just enough in her pocket to pay her fare—part of her plan-for-every-contingency strategy when she'd gotten ready for the interview—but when she looked behind her, she saw Noah cursing and trying to change a twenty to get a token. She suspected he would have leaped the turnstile, if there hadn't been a cop right there, watching him. Noah waved her on. "Go! I'll catch up."

Victoria ran down the tiled floor, weaving in and out of the crowds, barely aware of her surroundings, of the rushing trains, the volume of noise. Nothing seemed to register in her brain but helping Noah and reaching Justin.

The crowd parted as she reached the lower level, revealing the familiar red shirt ahead of her. She ran faster, clutching Charlie so tight she was sure he couldn't breathe. A few feet away, Justin leaped onto an Orange line inbound train, cramming into the jumble of people aboard. Victoria followed, slipping in just as the doors whooshed shut behind her. Too late, she saw Noah running to catch them, but ultimately ended up left behind, standing on the platform, bereft and worried.

The train jerked out of the station. As it picked up speed, Victoria shook off the rain, swept it off of Charlie's fur, then looked around. As she did, she became painfully aware of the claustrophobic feel of the small train car. The conflicting scents of wealth and abject poverty, the rising chatter of multiple conversations, the jostling bodies staking claim to a particular seat, handrail, exit. Each element compounded, one on top of the other, loading onto her chest in tiny, immovable mountains. She reached out, clutched one of the silver rails, her grasp so tight it turned the muscles in her arm to steel rods.

She closed her eyes, opened them, swaying as the car whipped around a curve, plunging the interior into black nothing, then just as quickly, light.

The conductor's voice came on, announcing the next station, the word "State" coming out in one flat syllable.

Justin. She had to find Justin. Before the train stopped and he slipped away. Again.

Victoria drew in a breath, trying in vain to still her thundering pulse. She scanned the crowd, a sea of blondes, brunettes, hats, bald heads. At first, she didn't see him, and panic gained a solid footing in her mind. Had she gotten on the wrong train, had he gotten off before the doors shut?

She forced herself to let go of the bar, to squeeze through the cluster of riders. Outside the windows, the tunnel rushed by in a terrifying blur of stained concrete.

It was as far from her house as Mars was from South Dakota. Every instinct within her said to flee.

But to where? Jumping off the train wasn't a possibility. Cowering in a corner wasn't, either. Noah needed her, Justin needed both of them, and for that, she had to get a grip and move forward.

She held tight to Charlie, murmuring "excuse me" as

she pushed past a teen couple who were doing things most people only did in a motel room.

Then, finally, pressed against the steel rails that lined the rear exit, was the boy. Thin, wet and dirty, he stared out at the dingy gray walls of the tunnel. Something lonely and haunted seemed to lurk in his eyes, as if he were searching for something that couldn't be found.

The urge to help him, to erase that look, whisked away the fear that had locked her in place. "Justin?" Victoria asked, zigzagging the rest of the way to him.

For a split second, she saw the vulnerable boy in his face, a hint of a smile when he recognized the dog, then a scowl took over his features. A hint of Noah's features resided in his eyes, the shape of his mouth. "Who are you?"

"I'm a friend of your uncle's."

The scowl deepened, intensified by teenage attitude. "I don't have an uncle." His gaze cut away, but not before Victoria saw a glimmer in those hardened green eyes.

"Noah has been looking for you. You have no idea how worried he's been about you."

Justin let out a snort.

"He wants to help you."

Justin wheeled around, crimson spotting his pale cheeks. "I don't want any help, lady. So just get off my back. You and my uncle."

So much for the Disney happy ending she'd envisioned. Above her, the announcer said "State" again in the same flat monotone, just as the brakes began to squeal, bringing the train into the next station. Justin coiled tight as a spring, ready to bolt when the doors opened.

"You may not want help now," Victoria said, digging

into her pockets, shuffling the dog from one arm to the other, earning a protesting yip, "or want to talk to Noah, either, but take this—" She handed him two twenties, money she had tucked in her pocket that morning for a shoe splurge after her job interview. "It's enough for cab fare and something to eat for the next couple of days."

Wariness made him hesitate, but then he snatched the dollars out of her hand and stuffed them into the back pocket of his jeans.

At the same time, the doors whooshed open and people spilled forward onto the platform. Justin muttered something that sounded like "thanks," then dashed out of the car, immediately blending into the crowd.

Victoria ran after him, at the same time digging in her purse, looking for the ad she'd written for the newspaper, the ad she'd never sent, for a room she'd changed her mind about renting. She latched onto the slim piece of lined notebook paper, then looked around. For a second, she couldn't find him and panic clawed at her throat.

Red sweatshirt. Look for the red sweatshirt.

The flash of crimson caught her eye, like one color element in a black-and-white movie. She brushed past the other commuters, colliding with briefcases and purses, and caught up to Justin, stuffing the paper into his hand before he could refuse it. "This is my address and phone number. Your uncle is staying there—"

But Justin had already turned away, hurrying off into the bowels of the busy subway station, out of her reach.

Victoria worried over the encounter in her mind, wondering if there was something she could have done different, said different, that would have resulted in Justin staying instead of taking off again. She was no expert with children, with other people. She'd worked purely on instinct.

All she could do was pray those instincts had been right.

"Where is he?"

She wheeled around. Noah stood behind her, out of breath and flushed with exertion. A second Haymarket train stood in the station, clearly Noah's conveyance, sadly a few minutes too late. "He left again."

"You didn't stop him? Hold onto him? How could you let him go?"

She parked a fist on a hip. "What did you want me to do? Make a citizen's arrest?"

He let out a curse, then kicked at a bottle cap on the tiled floor. "No. I just wanted…"

"A miracle?"

Noah shook his head. "I gave up on those a long time ago."

"You never know when one might happen, Noah," she said gently, reaching for him. "Justin could—"

He jerked away from her. "Listen, I know you have this Pollyanna view of life but in the real world, it doesn't work like that. Kids get addicted to drugs. They run away. They die. And there's nothing you can do to stop it."

And then, he stopped, swiping a hand across his face. "I'm sorry, Victoria. I'm frustrated with Justin and the legal system and myself. I'm taking it all out on you." He took her hands in his, searching her eyes for forgiveness. "I mean it. You've done so much for me, and having you here has meant more than I can say."

The admission caught her off guard. She dipped her head, suddenly feeling shy, vulnerable. "It was nothing."

"No, Superwoman," he said, tipping her face up to meet his, "it was incredible. You were incredible, dodging those crowds, hopping trains like Arnold Schwarzenegger."

She laughed. "You're the hero here. I'm just the sidekick."

"You are more than that. Much more."

She felt his words settle against her heart, taking up permanent residence. How she wanted to hold onto them. Hold onto him, to this moment.

But reality was intruding, in the form of another train rushing in and groups of people unabashedly eavesdropping. "We should go outside."

Noah nodded, the moment between them broken. As they turned to go, he looked back down the passageway Justin had taken. "How are we going to find him?"

She smiled. "He's going to find us. When he's ready."

Then she took Noah and a shivering, wet Chihuahua back home.

CHAPTER TWELVE

THEY searched for hours in the rain, but Justin was nowhere to be found. Noah updated the police, tried his brother, but didn't get an answer, and finally yielded to Victoria's advice that they go home, get dry and get some rest before going back out again to look.

As soon as they got back to the house, Charlie leaped out of Victoria's arms, shook off the rest of the wet and went to curl up on the carpet in Noah's room, clearly wanting nothing more to do with the humans who had subjected him to a torrential downpour.

Quiet descended over the house. This time, however, the silence didn't seem so suffocating, so lonely. It was a comfortable silence, borne from the knowledge that someone else was there.

Noah.

Outside, the rain continued to fall in heavy sheets that rolled across the street in tiny waves. The storm pelted the house, making little pitter-patter sounds on the wood shingles.

Victoria shivered, wrapping her arms around herself. "I'm freezing. Do you want some tea? I'm going to make a pot."

"Sure," Noah said, from his stance by the window. He'd been looking through the glass for the last hour, worried, she was sure, about Justin out in this downpour.

She made the tea, added some of the store-bought cookies to a plate, then set the snack on the kitchen table. As she sipped from her mug, Noah joined her, the troubled look still on his face.

"He'll be okay," she said, reaching out to clasp his hand with her own.

"Hey, your hands are like ice," Noah said, putting his other one on top of hers. "Are you okay?"

"Just cold." She shivered. "I don't know why. I turned up the heat, had some tea, but I'm still cold. Maybe the furnace is on the blink again."

Noah placed a palm against her forehead. "You're burning up. What you need to do is get into bed."

"No, no, I'm fine. Really." She smiled, just to prove it. "Besides, didn't you promise to give me a mock interview tonight, to get me ready for Friday?"

He rose, drawing her up with him as he did. "All that can wait. Tonight, you need to take care of yourself. You probably caught a cold in all that rain."

"I'm fine. I—" She cut herself off, let out a sneeze, then tried to finish the sentence. "I'm hard-dy code at all."

"Uh-huh."

"Besides, I was going to make some brownies for Mrs. Witherspoon's birthday tomorrow. I haven't even checked today's classifieds for a job, either, in case that interview doesn't work out. There are dishes in the sink, laundry in the washer. I have things to do, Noah. I can't be going to bed in the middle of the day." But the words all came out in a jumble of hard consonants, muffled by the congestion in her sinuses.

He touched her cheek. "Victoria, the world won't stop spinning without you."

"But what about cleaning up from dinner? Getting the truck? You need—"

"What I need is for you to go to bed. Now." Before she could protest again, he bent down, scooped her up in his arms and started toward the stairs.

"Noah!"

"You've taken care of everyone else your whole life. Let someone else take care of you for a change."

She should have protested. Insisted on staying up. It was, after all, just a cold. But there was something about being wrapped in his protective arms and hearing the words "take care of you" that kept Victoria from voicing a single objection as Noah carried her up the stairs, into her room and laid her gently on the bed.

"Where are your pajamas?" he asked.

"I can certainly—" She saw the determination in his eyes. Surely he didn't intend to…? Nevertheless, she found herself pointing across the room. "Bottom right drawer. But—"

Her objections were cut off by Noah crossing the room, pulling out a pair of pink flannel PJs, then returning to her side.

"I can…"

"Let me." He looked down at her, and in his gaze, she saw something that went way beyond caretaking. He wanted her.

That feeling was certainly mutual.

Noah reached up, drifted his hand along the back of

her cheek, his touch so tender, so gentle, she nearly cried. "Thank you," he whispered.

"For what?"

"For helping me. For going after Justin. For just—" he drew in a breath, let it out "—being in my corner. You have no idea how much that means to me."

She almost said something trite like, "Anytime," voicing words that would defuse the situation, take the coiling, tightening tension between them down a notch. Or ten.

She had spent her whole life being afraid. Of the outside world. Of experiences. And recently, of getting close to anyone again.

No more. If there was one thing Victoria Blackstone was done feeling, it was fear.

"It's easy to do," she said, opening her heart another few inches, letting him in, "when you care about someone."

There. The words were out. Granted, they weren't those special three little words, but they were more than she had ever said to a man in her life.

"Victoria," Noah said, her name slipping from his lips in a whisper. He leaned forward, his gaze never leaving hers, adding an intensity, a depth, that took the moment into another realm. When he kissed her, his touch was as gentle as a cashmere blanket.

Then he drew back, his gaze still on hers, heat multiplying in those dark green eyes. "Let's get you ready for bed."

All she could do was nod.

Working slowly, he slipped her navy suit jacket off one shoulder, then the other, letting it puddle behind her on the bed. Then, his eyes met her own, asking a question, waiting for the answer.

She tamped down her hesitation and nodded again, then, fascinated, watched his hands, the strong, capable hands of a man, beginning to work the tiny pearl buttons that trailed down the front of her shirt. One after another, he slipped them out of their fastening holes, the fabric parting just enough to let a whisper of a draft tingle against her skin.

She had never been naked with a man before. Never had a man see her in anything more revealing than a one-piece swimsuit. At first, she wanted to cover up, to block his view, but as Noah parted the two panels of her shirt, she didn't feel a moment's hesitation or shyness. With him, it simply felt…right.

He waltzed his fingers slowly down her skin, following the path of the thin satin straps, then over her shoulders, reaching into the fabric and slipping the cream blouse down and off her torso. It, too slid down her skin and landed in a heap on top of the jacket. Room air whispered over her, raising tiny goose bumps.

Nervousness made her shiver. Would he like what he saw? She pressed a hand to her throat, then slowly, removed it, allowing Noah to look.

He smiled. "Lace. A nice surprise." He paused, his hand drifting over her skin, reverent, slow. "Oh, Victoria, you're so beautiful. So, so beautiful."

Coming from any other man, the words might have seemed trite, overused. In Noah's voice, however, she could hear honesty. The compliment soared through her, pushing her shyness to the side.

He cupped her face, then brought his lips to hers

again. This time, his kiss held more than a light touch. It held promises, of what could come later, of exactly how he would take care of her.

As he kissed her, his hands drifted down, over her arms, drawing her closer, into the circle of warmth from his body. She curved into him, tipping her head up, sliding her legs across his lap. What had started out as a sweet gesture was quickly building into something heated, fiery. Desire for him multiplied inside her, building like a storm fed by warm waters.

Victoria slid her palms beneath his T-shirt, meeting hard, defined muscles that bunched as he moved to pull her closer. She tugged the soft cotton up, then over his head, pausing to marvel at the solidity of him, the width of his chest. She had seen men's naked chests every summer on the beach, but none of them had ever been in her bedroom, nor had any of them ever been so close she could place her palms against his warmth. "You're incredible," she said, tracing the planes and muscles, amazed at how he could be so hard and so tender, all at the same time.

He groaned, then scooped her up, turning her as he did, her legs slipping naturally into the spaces on either side of his. His fingers went to the button and zipper at the back of her skirt, fumbling a moment before getting them undone, releasing the fabric from her waist.

Thirty years of living on the outskirts of a normal life exploded within her, fueling a powerful want. Driven by nature, by instinct, zinging desire through every ounce of her body. Her hands went up to cup his face, to pull his mouth closer to hers, to ask, without speaking, for more.

For him.

His hands roamed her back, then over her shoulders. He hooked a finger under each of the thin, white straps, hesitating only long enough for her to draw in a breath of anticipation.

"Noah," she said, the word a moan. "Please…" she added, not knowing what to ask for, knowing only that she needed him. Now.

He murmured her name between their lips, then trailed kisses along her jaw, down her neck, tasting every inch of skin on the sweet, torturous journey to her breasts.

"Oh, Noah…" The words left her, caught in a dizzying tornado of sensations.

He paused, looked up, his fingers danced along her jaw, his eyes watching her with warmth and something she was sure echoed her own feelings. "How did I end up with a woman like you?"

She laughed, the sound throatier than any laugh that had ever escaped her throat before. "I think you can blame it on your truck."

He chuckled. "I've never been so glad to break down."

"And I've never been so glad to rent out a room." Anticipation pooled in her veins.

His thumb traced her lower lip. She opened her mouth, tasted the tip of his finger, wanting more. He shut his eyes for a brief second. "Oh, hell, Victoria, what are you doing to me?"

"Nothing more than I hope you're going to do to me." She dipped her head, a flush filling her cheeks. She should tell him. It was only fair. "Noah, I think you should know that I've never…well, never been with a man."

His eyes widened, then the pieces of her life that she'd shared with him clicked into place in his mind. "Never?"

She grinned, using humor to offset what to her was beyond embarrassing. For God's sake, she was thirty years old. She should have had more experience by now. "I told you, I didn't get out much."

"That's nothing to be embarrassed by," he said, reading her mind. His fingers trailed along her cheek, easy as a feather. "It's a gift, a treasure. One you should save for someone special."

She cupped his face. "You, Noah, are someone special."

He looked away for a long moment, then back at her. When his gaze met hers again, the heat had left it, leaving the green more bittersweet. "I want to, believe me when I tell you I want to…" He slid his finger along her jaw.

"But?" Victoria held her breath, not sure she wanted to hear the answer.

"But you're the kind of woman who deserves more. More than one night, more than a kiss in the morning from a man who's not going to hang around long enough to—"

"Marry me? I don't want that, Noah. I don't want anything like that."

"You should," he said, his voice gentle, "because you deserve that. You're too good, Victoria, too good for a man like me. A man who's just going to leave." Then he slid off the bed, tugging her back into a sitting position. He picked up the pink flannel pajama top and slipped it over her shoulders, drawing it closed to cover her. A moment later, she was tucked into bed, a blanket drawn up to her chin. "I can't commit to anyone, even you, because there's so much unfinished business in my life.

Someday…" His voice trailed off, then he shook his head. "Get some rest," he said gently, then left the room.

Leaving Victoria alone, feeling both touched and confused.

Noah headed out to the kitchen, forcing his feet to move forward while his entire brain wished it could have stayed behind and finished what they had started.

He crossed to the sink, gripping the cold porcelain on either side. "Oh, hell," he muttered.

He'd done the right thing, he knew that. He just wished it didn't make him so miserable.

On the counter, his cell phone began to ring, the vibrations causing it to dance across the smooth surface. He flipped it open, growled out a hello.

"Mr. McCarty? It's Larry, from the garage. Your truck is ready. I'm real sorry I didn't have it done sooner, but I had to wait on that part. Anyway, to make it up to you, I'll run it out there."

"Oh, yeah, great. I appreciate it." The words came out of his mouth, but he didn't feel them. He should have been excited. His truck was ready. He could leave anytime he wanted. Leave, before he watched his nephew take off for good. Leave, before he broke Victoria's heart. Leave before he saw all of his mistakes stacked up like bricks, leaving even more people in their wake.

Leave, before he considered staying here, with the white picket fence, the claw-foot dining room table and the woman who had made home a reality.

A little while later Larry came and exchanged the keys for a check, before taking off in a brightly painted truck that had Larry's Garage: Repairs Or Rust: We Do

It All emblazoned on the sides. Noah stood in the kitchen, feeling the weight of his keys in his hands.

There was nothing holding him here now. Nothing except himself.

He looked around the kitchen, at the anachronistic furnishings and appliances. And realized that if he left now, all he'd be doing was running away again.

From a truth he hadn't yet faced.

CHAPTER THIRTEEN

VICTORIA heard the truck start up and pull out of the driveway a few hours later. Noah had left.

She laid there in her bed for a long time that night, telling herself it was all for the best, before finally succumbing to the cold bug and falling into a deep, dreamless sleep. When she finally awoke, it was to the scent of coffee and toast.

And the sight of Noah, standing in her room, a loaded breakfast tray in his hands. A single zinnia, one of the lone stragglers left in her flower beds, peeked its big round face out of a slim vase. "Your breakfast, milady."

"You're here." There was no hiding the surprise in her voice.

"I left, for a while," he said. "Just to go looking for Justin. But I came back, in time to take care of you."

She laughed, unable to deny the happiness rocketing through her at the thought that he had come back. "Why thank you. I had no idea room service was this good here."

"Wait till you get the bill." He grinned, laid the tray across her hips, then took a seat on the edge of the bed, careful not to dislodge her breakfast. "My truck is ready," he said. "Larry even brought it by last night while you were sleeping. He was just as you said, good at his job and honest with his prices."

"Oh." That meant he was leaving. She sipped from her coffee, swallowing back the disappointment. "Thank you for bringing me breakfast before you left."

The last three words were more question than statement. They hung there, in the room, waiting for an answer. Victoria shouldn't want him to stay. She had her own life to live, a life that didn't need a man in it. At least, not now.

Still, a tiny part of her wanted to rewrite the plan, to make some room for Noah. For more kisses, more sharing. Would it be such a bad idea?

Was it possible for her to have her independence—and a relationship, too?

"And, I thought it was about time I explained a few things to you." He drew in a breath, stared at the coffee in his cup for a long second. "I need to tell you about myself, about the way I grew up. Or rather, the way I finished growing up."

She nodded. "Okay."

He turned and smiled at her. "See, that's what I like about you. No questions asked. Just…okay."

She shrugged. "I treasure my privacy and wouldn't dare intrude on someone else's."

He shook his head. "I have never met a woman like you. A woman who didn't put expectations on the table. Who just…accepted me, what I do for a living. Even a few of my faults."

She fingered the handmade quilt that covered the

bed, tracing the lines that ran between pale yellow and green strips of fabric. "I guess maybe that's because I know what it's like to be left out."

"Because growing up like you did, you were basically shut out of the world."

She nodded, amazed at how he'd gotten at the truth in a single sentence. "Yeah."

He gave her a soft smile of understanding, then went on. "My plan, when I left Rhode Island last week, was to become a hermit."

She laughed. "Trust me, it's not all it's cracked up to be."

He grinned. "Out of all the houses I could break down in front of, it had to be the one with the woman who was doing her damnedest *not* to be a hermit, huh?"

"Must be karma."

"Yeah, I think it is." He pushed the plate of buttered toast her way. "Eat, and I'll talk."

"I'm fine, Noah."

"That's why you're still talking like a duck this morning, right?"

"Gee, thanks."

"You look like a beauty queen—" his hand rested briefly against her face "—but your voice tells me you still have a cold. So eat up."

She did as he asked, waiting for him to continue. For a long time, the only sound in the room was the crunch of toast.

"When I was a kid, my dad was…well, let's just say he wasn't the best role model. I have no idea what my mom saw in him when she married him, but it must have been something. Either way, whatever that something was, it was long gone by the time me and my little brother Robert came along."

He took a sip of coffee, then went on. "He wasn't abusive, but he was a cheater. And not just an ordinary cheater, who'd hide the receipts beneath his socks in the top dresser drawer. He was pretty flagrant about it, as if he felt it was his right to have a few affairs. Stress relief, he called it." Noah shook his head, clearly disgusted. "He broke my mother's heart a hundred times over. She tried like hell to keep the family together, because back in those days, a woman didn't just head off to the courthouse. In the end, though, my dad ran off with some woman he met in a bar, and the family, such as it was, fell apart."

Her heart ached for the boys they had been, for a childhood that had, in many, many ways been so much worse than hers. "What happened to you? And Robert?"

"Robert handled it okay. He stepped in, became the man of the house, even though he was the youngest. That's how he was, always the responsible one, the one who got good grades, remembered to take out the trash on Tuesdays. He even joined the Army on the day of his eighteenth birthday. Me, I left home when I was fifteen."

"Why?"

"At the time, I thought I was doing my mother a favor. You know, reducing the number of mouths she had to feed. But really, I was going to find the old man, have it out with him, tell him what I thought of him. I was a teenager. Thought I could conquer the world." He chuckled. "Hell, ninety percent of the teens I've met through my work think the same thing. It's something in the hormones, I swear. Anyway, I got through most of the United States in a couple of years. Took until Oklahoma before I found my father."

"He'd never kept in touch?" She sat back, amazed at a father who could let his child go. Her parents, as protective as they had been, had always loved her. Of that, she had never had doubts.

Noah snorted. "He never thought to put a dime in the mail for my mother and his kids. Once he was gone, he was gone."

"What happened when you saw him?"

"Nothing." Noah looked away, pausing for a long second. "And I think that was the worst part. My dad acted like he'd just seen me the day before, not two years earlier. Pretended everything was just fine with him and the woman of the week, like I should just move on in and create a little family again. When I told him I couldn't, he gave me ten bucks and sent me on my way. Did his paternal duty for the year." He let out a snort.

She laid back against the pillows, reeling from the information, sympathy tightening in her chest for Noah, and the boy he never got to be. "I can't imagine anyone doing that."

"Believe me, there are more people out there like that than you want to know."

"Oh, Noah, that's so sad."

"No, that's life, for lots of these kids." His voice was tinted with defeat, telling her he'd seen far too many children who had walked in the same shoes as he had. She understood Noah a little better now, and why he shut himself off from feelings. If he let in the emotions with a job like that, he'd be drowning in it.

"Was it that way for Justin, too?"

"No, and that's what made it so much worse," Noah said. He ran a hand through his hair, displacing the brown waves. She wanted to reach out, make it all right, even as she knew she couldn't. Noah sighed, then continued. "He grew up normal. With everything he wanted. I mean, Robert traveled for the Army, but he always made sure he had someone that could watch Justin, if he had to go overseas. Even with me and Robert watching him like a hawk, he went off the path." He shook his head. "I thought I knew enough to protect him, to keep him from doing that."

She put the pieces together, of everything he had told her, and realized the man across from her was far more complex than she had realized. Her hand laced through his, giving support as much as comfort. "Because you went through it yourself."

"I'd been there," he said, nodding. "I knew how hard it was on the streets. I slept in boxes, on storefront stoops, in shelters. I worked jobs I hated, ate food that people tossed away, turned in cans to get a cup of coffee that would have to last me all day when I had no money, no work."

She moved the tray to the floor, then slid across the bed, wrapping her arms around Noah. He leaned into her, accepting the embrace. She pressed her head to his chest, listening to the steady thump of his heart. A heart that had been broken untold times by loss. "Oh, Noah, I'm sorry."

For a long time, she just held him, wishing she could make up for all of it, could repay the boy who had lost so much. He seemed to draw from her touch, his hand on her back steady and warm.

Finally he drew back. "As awful as all of that was, it taught me what I needed to know to work with these kids. To help them."

"And you did, I'm sure."

He shook his head. "No, not if I couldn't save my own family." His gaze went to the window, to the inky, wet darkness outside. The rain storm was once again in full swing. Victoria clutched his hand with her own, trying to share his burden, to let him know he wasn't alone in his worry. In the silence, the connection between them seemed to intensify, raising above simple attraction and blossoming into something far deeper.

Something that felt a lot like love. The feeling didn't scare her, as she'd expected it would. Instead of enforcing the prison walls around her life, it began to break them down, brick after brick.

"Who saved you, Noah?" she asked.

A smile stole across his face, filled with the memory that had been the basis for all his future choices. "A businessman named Will Brennan. I went into his store one day, offering to do anything he needed. Sweep the floor, wash the windows, stock the shelves. I just needed work, money. He must have seen past the young and cocky, because he gave me a job, a listening ear, and within a few weeks, enough smarts to go back home, finish high school and go on to college."

"He must have been a heck of a guy."

"He was. For some reason, he saw something special in me, and that made me believe it, too. I went into juvenile work, as a way to pay him back. For helping me find my place in the world." Again, Noah's gaze went to the window, and with it, she knew, his thoughts.

"Justin is going to be okay, Noah."

"I wish I could be sure."

"He has my address, more than enough cab fare to get here. And he knows you're worried. He'll come around."

Noah swung his gaze back to her. "How can you know that for sure?"

"Because I looked into his eyes, Noah, and I saw someone who was lost." She had seen that in Noah's eyes, too, on that very first day when he'd been standing on the other side of her picket fence. For Justin, she was praying two twenty dollar bills and a slip of paper would be enough to bring him back. Noah, she knew, needed a lot more than that. He needed to forgive himself.

She knew from experience how impossible that mountain was to crest.

"When he's ready to be found, he'll come around," she said.

"You don't understand these kids, Victoria. They hook up with gangs, believe they're a family. And once they do that, most of them, they never come back." The words were pained, filled with the other defeats, the ones Noah wasn't talking about. After the past year of watching her parents die, Victoria also knew that feeling of loss, of futility.

"If that's the case, then why did Justin follow you to Boston?" she asked him.

The question rocked him, sending a shiver of hope up Noah's spine. Why *had* Justin come to Boston? And most of all, how had he known that his uncle was here, not in Maine or Rhode Island or in any of the cities along the way?

"It could have been a coincidence," Noah said. Pragmatism, he had learned, was always a wiser course than hope.

"And it could have been on purpose, Mr. Glass is Half Empty." She took his hand in her own, giving it a comforting squeeze. "Trust him."

"*Trust him*? After all he's done? He's been on the streets, doing God knows what to survive—"

"Just like you did."

"Yeah, but—"

"That wasn't any different," Victoria said. "And there's no reason why the outcome has to be different, either. Just open your heart, Noah, and trust."

It was something he hadn't done in a long, long time. In his line of work, trusting too much usually resulted in disappointment. Troubled teenagers, he knew all too well, let people down.

Before he could think, Victoria had slipped into the space between his arms. She held him tight, tight enough that he felt like he could let go, release the worries that had sat on his back for so long.

She was there for him, in every way. From the conversation to her touch, everything about this woman said she cared, she worried, right alongside him. He had never in his life known a woman who intuited what he needed—and then gave it to him.

Someone like Victoria was rare. A gift to be treasured.

A woman to be loved.

Whoa. That was going down a path he'd never envisioned for himself, not given his past. For a moment, he held her against him and wondered…what would it be like to be with her, like this, every day? To have her listening ears, her soulful eyes, her tender touch?

To fall in love with her and take the biggest risk of all—get married and have their own children?

The thought flitted through his mind, taking hold, running mental pictures. Dreams of a future.

No. He wouldn't think about that. Not now. Not until he knew his nephew was safe.

Then…maybe, he'd open another door in his heart. The one with the kryptonite lock keeping it shut.

Noah drew in a breath, then laid his head on Victoria's shoulder and allowed himself to take one tiny step.

And trust.

CHAPTER FOURTEEN

CHARLIE took advantage of the human cuddle to devour the remaining toast, giving Noah an uppity swish of his tail as he darted off, the bread prize in his tiny jaws. Victoria laughed, Noah cursed the Chihuahua, but then ended up laughing along with her.

It broke the somber mood between them, adding a touch of lightness to a day that had contained altogether too much dark.

"You know, I think that dog is actually becoming normal," Noah said. "My mother is never going to forgive me for ruining him."

"He's been so great to have around, I've been thinking about getting a Chihuahua. Maybe after he's gone—" She cut off the words, the lightness erased from her face. She forced a smile back to her lips. "Anyway, someday, I'll have to get one of my own."

"I'm not usually big on pocket dogs myself," Noah said, avoiding the question of when he and the dog would be gone. "But Charlie has…grown on me."

At his feet, the dog perked up one ear, then the other and let out a yip. Noah bent down and ruffled the dog's ears. Charlie froze for a second, then relented to the tender touch and flipped onto his back. Noah chuckled. "Are you sure you didn't drug him?"

"No. Just told him really good things about you when you weren't around. I think it helped change his attitude a bit."

"You should go into PR. If you can convince Charlie—" His cell phone vibrated against his hip, cutting off his sentence. He gave Victoria an apology, then flipped open the metal lid. "Hello?"

"Noah, I only have a second." Robert's voice, rushed and panicked. "Tell me Justin's okay. I hate being all the way over here and not be able to do a damned thing. Tell me you've found him."

Noah hesitated. He didn't want to worry Robert any more than he already was. His little brother spent every day charging into danger zones and needed his wits about him.

But then Noah realized that being honest, with himself, with Victoria, had seemed to lift the burden, made it easier to share the worries about Justin. For too long, he'd kept too much to himself, thinking he was protecting his younger brother. It was time he stopped that, too. "I did find him. He's here in Boston. I don't know why or how he got here, but Victoria caught up to him on the subway."

"Victoria?"

"She's my…" Landlady didn't seem right. Friend was way too casual. Girlfriend sounded adolescent. "The woman I'm staying with," he said finally.

"And is he with you now?" The cell phone picked up some static, breaking Robert's voice into a staccato jumble.

"No. He took off again. But, Robert, he has the address where I'm staying. He has some money. He's going to come around. I know it."

"You're sure?" Robert's voice was pained, filled with hopes that had been dashed one too many times. He was depending on his brother to be right.

Depending on him one more time. This time, unlike when their father had left, Noah couldn't let Robert down. He absolutely couldn't fail.

Noah glanced at Victoria and drew strength from her, from the belief in him, in Justin, that was clear in her blue eyes. "Yes."

Static crinkled across the line again. "I'm going into a dead zone here, Noah. I'll call you again soon as I can get a connection. If you hear anything, *anything*—"

"I'll call. Don't worry, Bob. Just keep yourself safe."

The call cut off, lost in the ether.

Noah closed his phone, then ran a hand through his hair. "If I'm wrong—"

"You won't be," Victoria said.

He believed her, partly because he needed to and partly because her faith was so unswerving. His had been more than a little shaky in the last few months. But this woman, a stranger a week ago, had changed all of that.

"I should get back out there and start looking again," Noah said, rising. "I hate being so powerless. I can only imagine how hard it is on my brother."

Victoria's light touch on him again. He'd never known anyone who so easily touched another—and gave so much in a simple gesture. "He's probably hunkered down somewhere, waiting for the rain to stop.

Why don't you stay in tonight?" She smiled. "And you can try to win back your toothpicks."

He reached up, cradled her face in his palms, his thumb tracing the outline of her lower lip. "You are definitely the sensible one."

She drew in a shaky breath, her blue gaze never leaving his, and filled with anticipation, want and more. "I'm not sensible at all," she said, "especially when it comes to you."

"Neither am I," he said, then did what every ounce of his body had been wanting to do all day. He leaned down and captured her mouth with his own with a kiss that spoke not of a bedroom but of a bond, brought about by mutual need for someone who would listen and most of all, care.

They stayed in the house that night, refusing Mrs. Witherspoon's invitation to dinner, just in case Justin came by. Outside, the storm continued unabated, as if the heavens were determined to unleash everything in their arsenal.

As night fell, drawing its dark shade over the world outside, the intimacy between Noah and Victoria increased. Although desire for her coursed through his veins every time he came within five feet of Victoria, he noticed that the more time they spent together, the easier being with her was. It seemed as if he'd been here for years, as if he'd known her forever.

It was the kind of comfortable relationship Noah had thought didn't exist. It certainly hadn't been the kind he'd had with Melissa, or with any other woman he'd dated. Maybe it was the shared experiences of the last few days, or maybe it was a sign of something more.

Something meant to be.

After a late dinner, Noah sat down beside Victoria on the newly moved floral sofa, handing her one of the two glasses of wine in his hands. The quiet in the house, broken only by the ticking of the hall clock, seemed to wrap around them like a blanket. A blanket that was feeling too comfortable. Eventually he'd have to go back. To his job, his barely furnished apartment. He needed to know that when he did, she would be okay. "Victoria, I don't want my problems to make you put your life on hold."

She sipped at her Chardonnay and patted Charlie, who had apparently traded in his silk bed for a spot beside Victoria. "They haven't. In fact, all we've gone through in the last few days has given me a new direction of sorts. You know, I learned something that day in the subway."

"What?"

She sat back against the sofa, drawing her knees up to her chest. "That I have everything in me already to move forward with my life. I kept waiting for…I don't know, a dose of courage to drop from the sky. Remember *The Wizard of Oz* and the Cowardly Lion?" Noah nodded. "Well, like him, I already had everything inside me. I just needed to put it into action."

"As easy as that?"

She laughed. "No, not really. A little at a time. But a small step forward is better than none, don't you think?"

He marveled at her, this woman who had transformed her life in a few short days, taken chances some people never took. "I think you made huge steps forward. Navigating the Mass Transit system like a pro. Driving in the city, for Pete's sake. There aren't too many things more terrifying than that."

"You're probably right." She ran a finger around the rim of the glass, avoiding his gaze. "And I did one more thing I've been afraid to do."

"What's that?"

Fall in love with you, Victoria wanted to say. The words lingered on her lips, ready for a breath, a push to release them. "I, ah, rearranged the living room, remember?"

"I like the new setup. It's more…" His voice trailed off, unable to supply an adjective.

"Modern?" She laughed. "Hard to do, given what I'm working with, but I've called the Salvation Army to come and pick up some of the furniture on Thursday. It's time I gave my own stamp to things. Besides, that gives me an excuse to shop, which gets me out of the house, too."

He grinned. "A win-win all around, huh?"

"Yeah." She was winning at all of her goals, at her intentions of moving forward. She should be happy. But instead she was miserable.

She wanted her cake. And the handsome fork to eat it with, too.

Noah, however, clearly also intended to move forward. He hadn't mentioned Maine or going back to his job lately, but he also hadn't said he wasn't leaving. The last thing she wanted to do was stop him, to put a damper on another person's plans. She'd stayed here all these years because her parents had asked her to. Asked for her help.

She couldn't do that to Noah, too. He had his own plans, and she wouldn't keep him from those. So she'd keep it light, and at the end, when Justin was safe, she'd say goodbye and pretend she'd be just fine without Noah.

A performance that would likely make her eligible for an Oscar.

Charlie leaped up, prancing his little feet back and forth across the cushions. He sat back on his haunches, then looked up at her, expectant.

"I think he needs to go out," Victoria said, reaching past the anxious dog to put her wineglass on the table, out of reach of a hyper tail.

"I can do it." Noah began to rise.

"No. I…I need some fresh air." And a moment away from his face, his eyes, his hands, and most of all, the memories that looking at him awakened.

"Victoria," he said, rising, his hand on her arm. "Promise me something."

"What?"

"That you won't let me or my problems be the reason you stay in this house, that you put off going after a job or traveling to Germany or whatever it is you want to do."

"I'm not doing that. Really." *I'll still go*, she thought, *but with a broken heart*.

He gazed at her, his green eyes seeming to read something in hers that even she couldn't see. "If you say so. I just don't want to see your life get set aside because of me. Once I go back to—"

"It won't," she promised, cutting his sentence off because she couldn't hear it. Not now, not tonight. She pressed a quick kiss to his cheek, then headed for the front door, grabbing an umbrella on her way out to the front porch, Charlie's preferred venue. Inside the house next door, she saw Mrs. Witherspoon doing something to her walls with a feather duster and some paint. She waved at her neighbor, then opened the umbrella over Charlie and herself as they made their way down the stairs.

The dog gave her a dubious look on the last step, but she nudged him forward. "You'll be fine. I'm right—"

Her gaze caught something standing beside the hundred-year-old maple tree across the street. A red sweatshirt. A soiled backpack. Torn, dirty jeans.

Justin.

Victoria scooped the dog up, then headed to the other sidewalk, slowly, afraid that what she saw was a figment of her imagination. That he would take off running again at any second.

But he stayed rooted to where he was, rain cascading over his hunched shoulders. He had his hands in his pockets, his head covered only by the sweatshirt hood.

He looked cold. Wet. And like someone who needed a caretaker more than anyone she'd ever known. Victoria reached him, then extended the umbrella to include the boy, too. "You found it," she said.

"Yeah. Took the bus, then I walked."

"Want to come in?"

He jerked his head in the direction of the house. "Is my uncle in there?"

She nodded. "And so is some lasagna and a cherry pie."

His eyes lit up at the mention of the food, but then he shook his head. "I should go. I wasn't planning on staying. I just…" He shrugged, instead of finishing the sentence.

"You can go, after you get dry and something in your stomach," Victoria said. "I have an extra room, if you want to get some sleep."

Justin quirked a grin at her. "Room for rent, huh?"

She laughed, remembering the ad she'd stuffed into his hands in the subway. "Well, for you, the rent is pretty cheap."

"I don't have any money."

"All I ask is that you have a conversation with Noah."

"He's just gonna yell at me." Justin looked down the road, as if considering how fast he could be out of here.

"If he does, I'll cut him off from the pie."

A faint grin crossed Justin's face. He looked at Victoria's house, then at the rain flooding the streets. He shrugged. "All right. Something to eat. That's all."

"Okay. We'll start there."

Like she had with Charlie, Victoria made baby steps with Justin. A little at a time, and hopefully, before he knew it, he'd stop being afraid of the storm that awaited him inside the house.

When Justin walked through the door of Victoria's house wet, bedraggled and dirty, it was all Noah could do to keep from letting out a cheer and rushing to embrace his nephew. All the frustrations, all the disappointments of the last few years, disappeared the minute he saw Justin's face, filled with trepidation, but a little bit of hope, too.

Noah played it as cool as he could, striding toward the boy, then opening his arms and waiting a long, scary second for Justin to walk into the hug and return the gesture. He held the boy to his chest, feeling the solidity, the realness of him.

Justin was safe. He was here.

Over Justin's head, Noah sent a grin Victoria's way, mouthing a thanks. She smiled back at him, one of those thousand-watt smiles that rocked his heart.

"I'm glad to see you, Justin," Noah said. "Really glad."

Justin drew back, out of Noah's arms, and offered a one-shoulder shrug. Leave it to two males to play it so cool, not a single emotion was exchanged. "Yeah, me, too."

"You okay? Are you hungry? Tired? Do you need to borrow some clothes?" Noah started off in one direction, then returned, realizing he hadn't even waited for Justin's answer.

"Your girlfriend, uh, she's making me a plate," Justin said. "I'm all right. I don't need nothing."

Noah paused, searching Justin's eyes for the telltale signs that his nephew was still lost to the world of drugs. A huge sigh of relief ran through Noah when he saw Justin was clear-eyed, his steady gaze taking in his surroundings, albeit with the same specter of attitude as before. "Let me get you some clothes," Noah said. "You can take a shower and—"

"I ain't staying." The one-shoulder shrug again. "So? I'm okay. Just wanted you to see that."

The wall between them was still there, as thick and as impenetrable as ever. Noah had no idea how to loosen a brick, to get through to the boy and regain the relationship they'd once had.

"I have some food for you in the kitchen," Victoria said, entering the room, the one bright spot in the tension between the two males.

Justin loped off toward the kitchen, followed by Charlie, who trotted along merrily, pausing from time to time to look up at this new stranger in the house. Noah trailed behind, running through everything he'd learned in his career, hoping to find the words that would repair the damage between them.

The words that would keep Justin from ever leaving again.

He came up as empty as a gas tank with a six-inch hole.

By the time Noah reached the kitchen, Justin was already seated at the table, shoveling lasagna into his mouth so fast, it was clear he hadn't eaten in a long while. Over the boy's head, Noah caught Victoria's eye. She smiled at him, and when she did, he felt as if his entire world was put back on its center.

Someday, he'd have to go back to Providence.

But not today. Not now. For now, there was his nephew and Victoria. Beautiful, smart and supportive Victoria, whose very presence seemed to expand into the empty spaces inside him. She was too good to be true.

And he was treading very close to something permanent.

Victoria gestured to Noah to take a seat at the table, jolting him out of his thoughts. He did, half afraid Justin would bolt the minute he sat down. But his nephew stayed, probably because Victoria added a second helping to his plate. She also dished up three helpings of cherry pie, sliding one in front of Noah. He gave her a smile of gratitude, not for the dessert, but for something to do, something to fill the tense silence centered around his nephew.

Noah threw out the first ten questions that came to mind. The kinds that encompassed "Where have you been?" and "What were you thinking?" and then racked his mind for something nonconfrontational. It seemed like all his years on the job had deserted him.

"So, Justin, tell me, what was your favorite part of Boston?" Victoria asked, filling the gap.

Justin was so surprised by the question that he stopped eating and just stared at her.

"While you were visiting here, I mean. What did you like the best? Your uncle said it's a little different from Providence."

Justin paused, thinking. "The Aquarium, I guess. I didn't get to go in, but I liked the seals."

"I liked them, too. They really like to ham it up when people are watching."

Justin smiled. Actually *smiled*. "Yeah. One of them was, like, clapping and stuff when I watched him."

Noah stared at Victoria, carrying on a conversation with Justin about aquatic mammals, for God's sake. For a second, he wanted to stop her, to redirect them all to the more serious issues at hand. But then he noticed something.

Victoria's easy way and nonthreatening conversational topics had done the one thing Noah had never been able to do. Softened Justin up. And even better, made him open up.

If he hadn't thought she was amazing before, he sure did now. A bona fide miracle worker. The thought of staying with her, of seeing her like this with their own children, took root in his mind.

Later, Noah promised himself, maybe he would consider those thoughts. Consider a future.

The three of them chatted like that for a while, as if this were an ordinary day. Noah fidgeted, then got up and paced the floor, knowing eventually, he had to get to the hard stuff. "Justin," he said when there was a lull in the conversation.

His nephew turned toward him. "Yeah?"

"What are you doing in Boston?"

Silence descended over the room. After a minute, Justin shrugged and the attitude that had been lifted with seal chitchat returned. "I dunno. I got friends here."

Noah wanted to ask who the friends were, if they were members of that gang back in Providence, if they were homeless, or worse, criminal. But he kept it as nonthreatening as he could, trying like hell to pull his personal connection out of the conversation. "Did you know I was here?"

Another shrug. Justin averted his gaze.

If only getting him to talk about himself was as easy as getting him to chatter on about wild sea animals. There was something there, something Justin wasn't telling him. A detail being left out of the conversation. Every radar in Noah's body was tuned tight, looking for the missing clues.

"I want to crash for a bit," Justin said. He turned to Victoria. "You got a place I can sleep?"

"Yeah, sure." She gestured to him to follow her, then led him up the stairs toward the bedrooms. Noah went after them only long enough to lend Justin some of his clothes, then headed back downstairs and grabbed his cell.

Dan was his customary happy self when he answered the phone. "What the hell do you want?"

"Some information," Noah said. "And I'm sorry for waking you up."

"You didn't wake me up," Dan said. "You *interrupted* me."

He'd forgotten about the new woman in Dan's life, a wealthy divorcée who'd met him at one of the fundraising events. Dan said she called him her "walk on the wild side." Except for Dan's tacky leopard print tie, Noah didn't see how Dan and the word "wild" went together.

"Sorry, Dan. Listen, I found Justin…or rather, he found me."

"You're kidding me. Really? Hell, that's great. The kid okay?"

"Yeah. A little thinner but all right, far as I can tell. What he won't tell me, though, is why he's here. How he found me and what happened in Providence to make him bolt."

"Did you try asking him?"

"Very funny. You and I both know anyone between the ages of thirteen and twenty does Mute very well."

Dan roared with laughter. "Listen, there's nothing happening on the streets, so if he left, it had nothing to do with the gang. Maybe he was looking for something."

"Maybe," Noah conceded. "Listen, I'd appreciate it if you could look into this, see what else you can scare up from the regular sources. We must be missing something. I want to know exactly what made Justin bolt. Maybe—"

"I can't believe you narced me out!"

Noah turned and saw his nephew in the doorway, disbelief and betrayal etched all over his features. Dread sunk to the pit of Noah's stomach. "Justin, I was worried. I was just—"

"I came here, because I thought I could trust you. But, instead—" he let out a gust "—you thought about your job, not me. I'm still just another one of your cases, aren't I?" Then he turned.

And ran.

Justin was already out the door, plunging into the

rainstorm, his years on the track team powering his legs faster than Noah's. Noah ran hard, following him down the street, across lawns, through a small playground. His heart thudded violently in his chest, his lungs burned like someone had doused them with kerosene, but he kept going, putting every ounce of effort into closing the gap. Finally, as they rounded a pair of swings, Noah lunged forward and managed to catch up to Justin. "Don't run, Justin. Let me—"

Justin bent over, hands on his knees, inhaling deep gulps of air. "*You're* telling *me* not to run away?" He let out a snort. "Who do you think I learned it from?"

"What do you mean? If anything, I told you how hard life is on the streets, how much your family needs you."

"My family…" Justin shook his head, his gaze going to a swing that drifted idly in the storm. "They don't need me. My father is in Iraq, for God's sake, for a second time. He volunteered to leave me. My mother—"

"What about your mother?" As far as Noah knew, Justin's mother had taken off soon as she got out of the hospital from having him and never looked back. Robert had done the one-parent show for a long time.

"Nothing." He toed at the ground, loosening a chunk of sod. "Just drop it."

"Justin," Noah said, taking a step forward. His nephew backed up, making Noah freeze in his tracks. "What you said about your dad isn't true. He loves you and he needs you."

"Oh, yeah? Do the math, Uncle Noah. You ran away fifteen years ago and I was born the same year. My dad was supposed to be the responsible one, taking care of

Grandma, doing all the right things. And all he did was screw up by having me."

"That isn't true. Your father was…" Noah paused, searching for the right words. "Everything I wasn't."

"My dad needed *you* back then," Justin said, spewing back the truth in the direct way only a kid could, "and you weren't there. You were supposed to be the older one, the one who took care of him. And when *I* needed you—" He turned away, cut off the sentence.

"When you needed me," Noah said, realizing the unspoken end of Justin's sentence, the consequences of his hasty trip out of town, "I was gone, too. I'm sorry, Justin."

The boy didn't say a word, just worked at relandscaping the ground.

"Then why didn't you talk to me when you saw me in Boston? Why did you run?"

Justin's eyes met his, clear and frank. "Because," he said quietly, "I was afraid you'd do just what you did. Be a cop instead of my uncle. Why can't you trust me?" His eyes welled up and before Noah could respond, he turned on his heel and sprinted down the road.

Noah turned to run after him. Beneath his feet, the soggy grass held no traction for his sneakers. He took a step, then slid forward. Scrambling for purchase, he reached for the swing, but the slick metal links slipped through his grip and he ended up sprawled on the wet ground.

While Justin disappeared again.

Victoria had been wrong. Hope was a wasted emotion.

CHAPTER FIFTEEN

IT DIDN'T take long for Noah to realize the boy didn't want to be found and definitely didn't want anything to do with his uncle. Noah had screwed up, this time, probably for good. Justin wasn't coming back and there wasn't any point in staying here anymore.

"I'm leaving," he told Victoria a few minutes later. She'd followed him upstairs where he stuffed his belongings into the duffel bag. Charlie sat on his square of carpet and whined a protest.

"You're…leaving?" The shock, the hurt on her face made him want to take the words back.

"I'm not good at relationships, Victoria," Noah said, convinced more than ever now, after the encounter with his nephew that he didn't have what it took to be a husband, a father. Hell, he could barely be an uncle. "You deserve a lot better."

"Says who? You? Because I don't think you're exactly the best expert on yourself." She propped her fists on her hips, showing him another dimension, a stronger side, than he'd ever seen before.

"Don't you understand? I let my brother down. I did

it fifteen years ago and I'm doing it now. Only this time I'm doing it to the next generation. If that's not a clue that I should give up on this family thing, I don't know what is."

"I don't want to hear it, Noah." The harshness of her words made him take a step back. "You're a good man, whether you believe it or not. And you've helped dozens and dozens of kids."

"Victoria, you don't know what it's like in my job. The failure rate—"

"I talked to Dan," she said, cutting off his objections. "He called on Sunday, while you were working out some frustrations on Mrs. Witherspoon's latest project. And you know what? He only had the highest praise for you. He told me about that kid you saved, the one whose father had left him on a roadside when he was seven? He told me how you went and saw that kid every single day for a year, until he got on the right track. He's in college now, did you know that?"

Immediately the image of Brian Winters popped into Noah's mind. The first time he'd met him, the boy had been a too thin, terrified boy who didn't trust a soul for six months. "Yeah, but—"

"And the girl, the one who got pregnant at sixteen and then thought if she went to jail, it would be easier to give up the baby because she'd be forced to? You counseled her, too. You convinced her to stay straight, then you got her a home to live in, a job, a school that would help her with care for the baby. And what's she doing now?"

"Managing a Starbucks. Getting married in two months."

"Exactly. Would you say you didn't help them? Or

the hundreds of other kids whose files have crossed your desk?" She took a step closer, those vibrant blue eyes missing nothing in his. "You told me that you went into the juvenile justice system because you thought you could change the world. You may not have changed the entire world, Noah, but you sure as hell did make a difference in your corner."

He opened his mouth to refute that, but she put a hand up to stop him. "That is more than I have done in my entire life," she continued. "All I've done is change a living room. Big deal." Tears pooled in her eyes. "I envy you, Noah McCarty, because you have done the one thing I haven't yet—lived."

"You've got me wrong, Victoria. I don't live. I exist. I go in, do my job, hope like hell I don't screw up and then go back to my empty apartment because—" He shook his head, not finishing.

"Because it's easier to be alone than to open your world to someone else," she said, her words soft now, colored with care.

"Yeah."

Her smile was bittersweet. "Welcome to the club."

He grinned a little and shook his head. "We're quite the pair, aren't we?"

"A match made in heaven." The words were out before she could stop them, the meaning hanging between them.

But Noah didn't turn away. Didn't throw out a joke to take the tension down a notch, or ten. Instead he took a step forward, brushed a strand of hair off her face, then kissed her.

This kiss was so unlike the others, so soft, so tender,

almost reverent. She curled into him, her resolve to remain strong and independent, to prepare herself for his departure, melting.

"You are too good for me," he whispered, pulling back. Then he turned, grabbed his bag and left.

Noah pulled out of the driveway, a reluctant and complaining Charlie beside him, once again gnawing on the dashboard, as part of a one-Chihuahua protest.

Noah drove for a long time without thinking, refusing to replay the events of today in his mind. He was doing the best thing, for everyone.

Or at least that's what he told himself as he flicked on his directional, signaling for the 95 North exit. The road that led to Maine, to isolation, to a few days away from everything.

As he took the turn, he glanced in his rearview mirror and caught the reflection of the nighttime Boston lights. Then, he saw himself, a man who looked tired and defeated.

And an awful lot like his father had.

He might as well have rung a bell in his head. Noah pulled off the side of the road so quickly, it startled Charlie into obedience. The dog sat back on the seat, shook off the piece of foam hanging from his mouth and stared at his temporary owner.

In that mirror, Noah realized, was the exact same man who had run away from his life at fifteen and was doing it all over again.

He'd often told the kids he counseled that if hitting your head against a brick wall hurts, stop doing it. He was hitting the same damned brick wall all over again.

He'd run away from home, run away from commitment, run away from his job when things went south.

And even now, when he had a beautiful woman a few miles away, a woman he could easily love, he was driving down the road in the wrong direction.

Why?

When the answer came to him, it was so startling that it rocked him back on the torn vinyl seat. He'd studied kids all his life, but never, not even for a millisecond, thought to apply the information he'd learned to himself.

To why he'd been a runaway. Why he'd never come close to giving his heart to another person. And now he knew.

Because the last thing he'd wanted to be was his father's son.

Way to repeat history, McCarty.

He may not have cheated on Victoria, but he'd broken her heart just the same by not being there. By walking out on her. He'd done the same with his nephew, maintaining a professional distance when what Justin needed more than anything else was someone who told him he cared.

Beside him, Charlie barked, expectant.

"You're right, Charlie," he said, putting the truck back into gear and heading for the on-ramp. "Let's head on back."

For the first time since Noah had met the dog, Charlie scooted across the seat and lay down next to Noah, snuggling against his jeans. Noah chuckled. Maybe there was hope after all.

He got back to her house in record time, navigating the nighttime traffic like a NASCAR driver. He left the duffel in the truck, grabbed the dog and headed through the white picket fence and up the porch stairs. "Victoria," he called, pushing through the door. "Victoria!"

Silence.

He halted, listening, and then, he heard the sound of tears, coming from upstairs. With Charlie padding along beside him, Noah made his way up the stairs, passing his bedroom, then Victoria's, before arriving at a third.

The same plain maple furniture as in the other bedrooms dominated the space, but with a fine sheen of dust coating the finish. The air was stuffy, the wallpaper a thick, heavy floral, the bedding plain and neat. Her parents' room.

When he entered, she didn't look up, didn't move. He whispered her name, then wrapped his arms around her, as she had done with him so many times before. She turned within his embrace, pressing her face against his chest. His shirt dampened with her tears.

After a moment, she drew back.

She paused, drawing in a breath, releasing it. "You were right about what you said earlier tonight. I'm not moving forward. Not really."

"Oh, Victoria, I didn't mean—"

"No, don't." Her blue eyes met his, steeled with determination. "Don't let me take the easy way out. I thought I'd moved forward, but then I came up here—" she indicated the room "—and realized that moving a sofa, going to the grocery store and sending in a few job applications isn't really moving forward." She smoothed a hand across the quilted bedspread, straightening what was already perfectly flat. "I'm still here, Noah, doing what I do best. I'm a caretaker.

Craving a bowl of chicken soup? I'm the girl to call. Looking for a warm blanket? A hot cup of tea? Victoria to the rescue. Everyone has their talents, and mine, it seems, is being there for other people."

"There's nothing wrong with that. Look at all you've accomplished and changed about your life in the last few days."

"That's little stuff. *Really* moving forward means conquering the big fears." She bit her lip, then continued, pushing past the watery tears in her eyes, being the strong, determined woman he had grown to respect and care about. "When the people you love leave you…it does something to you. It makes you want to steel your heart against ever experiencing that kind of loss again. Because the pain—" and with that word, her voice cracked into tiny pained shards "—is so big and so deep and so consuming, that you start to think it's better to go through the rest of your life never, ever getting close to anyone again."

He knew that feeling, had known it since the day his father walked out on them. A father he had idolized as a little boy, before he realized where his father had been spending his evenings, before he was old enough to see the toll his father's continual indiscretions had taken on the family. "I know what you mean. I did the same thing after my father left us," Noah said. "After a while it became easier to hold onto that distance rather than close the space between me and other people."

"Which is why you treated Justin like a case, not a nephew," she said.

"Yeah." By boxing the boy in with the words of his profession, Noah had only driven him away. He knew now what he would say to Justin…if he ever got lucky enough to have a second chance. He prayed he would.

She studied his face. "Is that why you haven't done it, either?"

"Done what?" he asked, but he already knew the words that were coming next.

"Fallen in love."

Those three words hung in the air between them, laden with meaning, as heavy as ripe fruit. For a second, Noah felt like he could reach forward, pluck the pear of words and hold them tight.

"I—" Then he realized he hadn't, not really. Even with Melissa, he'd held a part of himself back, kept his heart protected. "No, I haven't. I guess because it's always been safer that way."

In their connected gazes, he saw an understanding of him, of his life, that only Victoria Blackstone could have had. This woman, who had been a physical hermit, afraid to experience life, in case it slapped her once again with loss. And then there was him, a social hermit, pulling away from other people with distrust and emotional distance, so he could shield himself against the very same thing.

They were similar beings, each trying like hell to stay alone on an island, not realizing how much that isolation had cost them—

Until they'd met each other.

"Me, too," she whispered. "And here, all this time, I thought it was because I'd spent too much time in this house, living like one of those crazy ladies with all the cats."

He chuckled. "Charlie doesn't get along with cats, so it's a good thing you didn't do that."

A fleeting smile crossed her lips. "I kept thinking that if I got out of here, went into the city, experienced things, that everything would change. That I'd suddenly figure out what I wanted for my life."

"And did you?"

She shook her head, the tears threatening again at the edges of her eyelashes. "No."

He brushed back the hair that had drifted over her eyes. "Maybe that's because you already are doing what you're meant to do."

"What do you mean?"

"Being a caretaker isn't such a bad thing, Victoria, especially when you have people like me who—what is it that you said?—need a worrier more than anyone you've ever met."

"Noah, I can't sit around all day and take care of people who come and live in my extra bedroom. I need more than that. I didn't find the answers outside this house, but I know damned well I need to get out of here. I can't go back to the way I was." She looked at him. "I want more."

"Then who says you can't look for a job that plays into your talents? Do you really want to be a receptionist?"

"Well, no."

"Then why aren't you doing what you love to do? Go into healthcare. Teaching. Or if you're a real glutton for punishment, the juvenile justice system." His hand drifted down her cheek. "We could use more people like you."

She thought for a minute, emotions playing across her face like the flickering of lights. "And here I always thought it was my parents who screwed me up by keeping me here all the time."

"Hey, we all blame our parents. It's a lot easier than looking in the mirror." Something he knew too well after today.

She laughed softly. "It wouldn't be so bad, to go into a job like that. I could do what I love to do, but be out of the house, in the regular world."

He grinned. "Another win-win."

"And then…" Victoria's eyes met his, tears glistening like crystals in the blue depths. But then she drew in a breath, this woman who, to him, was tougher than a mountain, and the tears were held in check. "My life will stop being as empty and lifeless as this space. If I really want to change my life, I have to get over the fear that if I let someone need me, they're just going to leave."

"Because the really scary stuff is loving other people," Noah finished, knowing he'd just learned that very lesson today, too.

"Yeah." She exhaled. "Loss is a part of life. But you know what? It teaches you to treasure the moments you do have."

Her words settled against his thoughts, making his memory replay the last few days. He realized the walls that he had erected so carefully over the years had started to crumble, bit by bit, since the minute his truck broke down in front of her house. He, too, was done with living an empty life.

"I think that's a damned good idea," he said to her, then pulled her to him. Against his chest, he felt the beat of Victoria's heart, steady and sure. He leaned down and kissed her. She tasted as sweet as honey, as pure as sunshine. His lips drifted over hers, memorizing every detail.

She wrapped her arms around his back, her palms flat and secure against his back, holding him as much as he held her. Then her tongue darted inside, dancing with his, teasing him like a siren.

Noah wanted this moment to last forever. He wanted to lock the door against the real world and just stay here, with this woman, this moment.

Forever.

He opened his mouth to tell her that, to confess that somewhere between the puffer fish and the rainstorm, she had captured his heart. But before he could, Charlie began to bark, frantic and loud.

Reality had intruded. With all the timing of a wedding crasher.

Noah and Victoria headed down the stairs, just in time to see the front door open and the cold, blustery wind usher in one prodigal nephew. "Justin!" Noah said, no longer holding back, but rushing down the last few stairs and grabbing his nephew into a hug that would have put a bear to shame.

"Whoa, Uncle Noah, I still gotta breathe." But the words lacked any punch and there was a slight smile on the teenager's face. "I came back," he said after a moment, "because you were… Well, you were right."

"I was right?" Noah hadn't heard that very often in his years of working with teenagers. "About what?"

He shrugged a shoulder. "About me needing people. You know, like my dad. I mean, I'm, like, almost a grown-up. But…I thought it might be cool if I stayed with you, if you still wanted me—"

"Hell, yes. I do."

The smile widened a bit. "Well, good. 'Cuz I really don't want to go back. To any of that."

Across the room, Victoria smiled.

"And I don't want to go back, either," Noah said, "to not having faith in you."

"You?" Justin asked. "You have more faith than anyone I know. Look at what you do for a living. I mean, you keep giving kids like me second chances and all we do is screw it up."

"No, I'm the one doing that," Noah said. "When I was a boy, my father left me and your dad. Your dad turned out to be the responsible one, but he left, too, in a way."

"Yeah, got on a plane for Iraq."

Noah could see the anger in Justin, the disappointment at his father taking the second tour. Later, there would be time to repair that bridge. "When my dad left, I lost faith in other people." Noah's gaze went to Victoria. "But mostly in me. Been doing it all my life, in one way or another. I got damned good at putting up walls. With you, the wall was my job. I became your probation officer, instead of your uncle. Threw services and lectures at you when I should have just loved you."

A flush filled Justin's face. This wasn't manly talk, but it was words that needed to be said. "Yeah, well, I haven't exactly been the most cooperative kid, either. I kept ditching you and my dad, because I felt like you were ditching me." He drew in a breath, toed at the floor some more. "You know that day in the woods?"

"Yeah."

"I went looking for my mother after that. Thought maybe she'd be the one who would, I dunno, love me and all that. But she didn't want me, either. Said she didn't want her new husband to know about her mistakes."

The words sliced a gash in Noah's heart. He knew that pain, that disappointment. "She's an idiot," Noah said.

Justin blinked.

"Because you're not a mistake."

Tears filled the kid's eyes, but he swiped them away with the back of his hand. He swallowed, hard, trying like hell to maintain his cool. Noah drew him into his arms once again. At first, Justin resisted, trying to maintain his masculine bravado, but after a second, he relented, and accepted the love of the one man who could understand what he'd been through.

"After that, you came looking for me, didn't you?" Noah said, realizing now what had brought Justin here. "And when I wasn't there—"

"I hitched a ride, following you."

"I'm sorry I wasn't there when you needed me, Justin. It'll never happen again, I promise."

Justin nodded. "Yeah. That'll be good."

Noah smiled. "Yeah, I agree." And then, in the silent language of males, he gave his nephew another hug, telling him he loved him in the gesture. Over the top of Justin's head, Noah's gaze sought out Victoria's in the other room.

And made another promise, this time to himself. As soon as he could, he was going to put his new operating-on-faith policy into action.

Later that night after an exhausted Justin had fallen asleep in one of the upstairs bedrooms, Victoria snuggled up against Noah on the sofa, her head in the comfortable, perfect place against his shoulder. "I'm glad it all worked out."

Noah placed a soft kiss on her forehead. "Me, too. Justin will need some counseling, some time to work out things with his dad when Robert gets back, but I feel like, for the first time, we're on the right track." Then he thought of something and rose. "Wait here, just one minute."

He headed for the stereo, a behemoth piece of furniture that was nearly as large as the sofa. He flipped through the 45s, and as he'd expected, the one song he'd wanted was sitting there, in a collection that would have made an eBay auctioneer drool dollar signs.

"What are you doing?"

He put the needle down gently on the record, then turned to face her. "Setting the mood."

She arched a brow. "The mood…for what?"

He crossed the room in three long strides, then lowered himself to his knees in front of her. "For asking you if I can stay here."

"Stay?" Victoria said, forcing her voice to remain casual, unconcerned. "As a boarder?"

"No. As a husband."

Shock made her mouth drop open. She tried to sputter out some response, but nothing came. In the background, the singer went on and on about loving his pretty baby.

"I'm done running," Noah said. "And it's all your fault."

"My fault?" A short, anticipatory breath escaped her. Of all the words she'd expected him to say, "husband" hadn't even made the list.

"I fell in love with this house. This beach, this town and most of all—" he cupped her jaw, waiting until her gaze was locked on his "—with you."

He was in love with her. He wasn't leaving. He wanted more than just a temporary room. A smile broke across her face, reflecting inside her heart. "You love me?"

"I love everything about you, from the way you make lemonade to the way you smile. But—"

She grinned, joy exploding in her chest. "There's always a but, isn't there?"

"This time, definitely." He traced the outline of her lip with his thumb, sending desire spiraling through her veins. "But when I stay here, I won't be renting out that room."

"You won't?" She swallowed the disappointment that threatened to spill into her voice. "Why?"

"Because I'm going to get my own place in Hough's Neck. Find work in the same field here, give Justin a new start in a new town. We both need that. But mostly, because I want you to have time to explore your options, Victoria, to see where you want to go, what you want to do with your life. And, I don't want you to feel in any way like you need to take care of me. I'm perfectly capable of taking care of myself."

Victoria laughed. "As long as you have a recliner, a TV and a fridge full of beer?"

"Hey, I might be adding a coffee table. That way, Charlie has something to gnaw on when he comes to visit." At that, the Chihuahua leaped onto the sofa, pranced around in a circle three times, then settled his tiny body right beside Victoria. Noah groaned.

"He only does that because you don't show him enough attention, you know. Show him you love him and then he'll be nice to you."

Noah moved in closer, his lips brushing against hers, taking anticipation to a whole new level. "How about I start with showing how much I love you?" The words were a sexy whisper between them.

"Sounds like a plan," Victoria managed to reply, then kissed him, a short, sweet embrace that promised more. "I love you, too, Noah."

"Even if I end up winning all your toothpicks?" he teased.

She smiled, the light in her eyes dancing with a joy that Noah hoped to see every day for the rest of his life. "I don't know about that. I've already been dealt the best hand I could hope for." And with that, Victoria gave the room in her heart to Noah. No other renters need ever apply.

Charlie, however, snuck his little body in between them and let Noah know, with a cold, wet, teeny nose, that he was to be included in this deal, too.

SAVE UP TO $30! SIGN UP TODAY!

The complete guide to your favorite
Harlequin®, Silhouette® and Love Inspired® books.

✓ Newsletter ABSOLUTELY FREE! No purchase necessary.

✓ Valuable coupons for future purchases of Harlequin,
  Silhouette and Love Inspired books in every issue!

✓ Special excerpts & previews in each issue. Learn about all
  the hottest titles before they arrive in stores.

✓ No hassle—mailed directly to your door!

✓ Comes complete with a handy shopping checklist
  so you won't miss out on any titles.

- -

SIGN ME UP TO RECEIVE INSIDE ROMANCE
ABSOLUTELY FREE
(Please print clearly)

Name

Address

City/Town   State/Province   Zip/Postal Code

(098 KKM EJL9)
                                    Please mail this form to:
            In the U.S.A.: Inside Romance, P.O. Box 9057, Buffalo, NY 14269-9057
            In Canada: Inside Romance, P.O. Box 622, Fort Erie, ON L2A 5X3
                    OR visit http://www.eHarlequin.com/insideromance

IRNBPA06R   ® and ™ are trademarks owned and used by the trademark owner and/or its licensee.

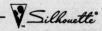

SPECIAL EDITION™

Silhouette Special Edition brings you a
heartwarming new story from the *New York Times*
bestselling author of *McKettrick's Choice*

LINDA LAEL MILLER

Sierra's Homecoming

Sierra's Homecoming
follows the parallel lives
of two McKettrick women,
living their lives in the
same house but
generations apart,
each with a special son
and an unlikely new
romance.

December 2006

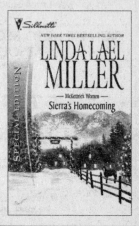

HARLEQUIN®

Blaze

New York Times bestselling author
Suzanne Forster brings you
another sizzling romance…

Club Casablanca—an exclusive gentleman's club where
exotic hostesses cater to the every need of high-stakes
gamblers, politicians and big-business execs. No rules
apply. And no unescorted women are allowed. Ever.
When a couple gets caught up in the club's hedonistic
allure, the only favors they end up trading are sensual….

DECADENT

November 2006

by

Suzanne Forster

Get it while it's hot!

Available wherever series romances are sold.

"Sex and danger ignite a bonfire of passion."
—*Romantic Times BOOKclub*

www.eHarlequin.com   HBSFI1106

Romantic
SUSPENSE

Excitement, danger and passion guaranteed

INTIMATE MOMENTS™

**Beginning in October
Silhouette Intimate Moments®
will be evolving into
Silhouette® Romantic Suspense.**

Look for it wherever you buy books!

Visit Silhouette Books at www.eHarlequin.com

SIMRS1006R

REQUEST YOUR FREE BOOKS!

2 FREE NOVELS PLUS 2 FREE GIFTS!

SILHOUETTE
Romance®

From Today to Forever...

YES! Please send me 2 FREE Silhouette Romance® novels and my 2 FREE gifts. After receiving them, if I don't wish to receive any more books, I can return the shipping statement marked "cancel." If I don't cancel, I will receive 4 brand-new novels every month and be billed just $3.57 per book in the U.S., or $4.05 per book in Canada, plus 25¢ shipping and handling per book and applicable taxes, if any*. That's a savings of over 15% off the cover price! I understand that accepting the 2 free books and gifts places me under no obligation to buy anything. I can always return a shipment and cancel at any time. Even if I never buy another book from Silhouette, the two free books and gifts are mine to keep forever.

210 SDN EEWU   310 SDN EEW6

Name	(PLEASE PRINT)	
Address		Apt.
City	State/Prov.	Zip/Postal Code

Signature (if under 18, a parent or guardian must sign)

Mail to Silhouette Reader Service™:

IN U.S.A.
P.O. Box 1867
Buffalo, NY
14240-1867

IN CANADA
P.O. Box 609
Fort Erie, Ontario
L2A 5X3

Not valid to current Silhouette Romance subscribers.

Want to try two free books from another line?
Call 1-800-873-8635 or visit www.morefreebooks.com.

* Terms and prices subject to change without notice. NY residents add applicable sales tax. Canadian residents will be charged applicable provincial taxes and GST. This offer is limited to one order per household. All orders subject to approval. Credit or debit balances in a customer's account(s) may be offset by any other outstanding balance owed by or to the customer. Please allow 4 to 6 weeks for delivery.

SROM06

Introducing…

nocturne™

**a dark and sexy new
paranormal romance line
from Silhouette Books.**

USA TODAY bestselling author
LINDSAY McKENNA
UNFORGIVEN

KATHLEEN KORBEL
DANGEROUS TEMPTATION

*Launching October 2006,
wherever books are sold.*

SNOCT

SILHOUETTE *Romance* ®

COMING NEXT MONTH

#1838 PLAIN JANE'S PRINCE CHARMING—Melissa McClone
When waitress Jane Dawson approaches millionaire Chase Ryder to sponsor her charity, she is thrilled when he agrees. Deep down she knows there is no chance sexy Chase will be interested in a plain Jane like her! But Jane's passion to help others is a breath of fresh air to Chase, and he soon realizes that Jane is a woman in a million, and deserves her very own happy ending.

#1839 THE TYCOON'S INSTANT FAMILY—
Caroline Anderson
When handsome business tycoon Nick Barron hires Georgie Cauldwell to help with his property development, they spend a few gorgeously romantic weeks together. Then Nick disappears! When he returns, it is with two young children and a tiny baby. Georgie knows she shouldn't fall in love with a man who has a family, but there is something about this family she can't resist.

#1840 HAVING THE BOSS'S BABIES—Barbara Hannay
Like the rest of the staff at Kanga Tours, Alice Madigan is nervous about meeting her new boss. But when he walks through the door it's worse than she could ever have imagined! She shared one very special night with him—and now they have to play it strictly business! But for how long can they pretend nothing happened?

#1841 HOW TO MARRY A BILLIONAIRE—Ally Blake
Cara Marlowe's new TV job will make her career—as long as nothing goes wrong. So it's bad news when billionaire Adam Tyler wants the show stopped, and worse that Cara can hardly concentrate with the gorgeous tycoon around! Cara wants Adam—and her job, too. Will she have to make a choice?